A Modern Daedalus

Tom Greer

A MODERN DÆDALUS

' . . . . such a yell was there
Of sudden and portentous birth,
As if men fought upon the earth,
And fiends in upper air.'
SCOTT.

BY

TOM GREER

GRIFFITH, FARRAN, OKEDEN & WELSH
SUCCESSORS TO NEWBERY AND HARRIS
WEST CORNER ST PAUL'S CHURCHYARD, LONDON
1885

A MODERN DÆDALUS

a

PREFACE.

LET no reader suppose that this book is the work of an enemy of England. On the contrary, though a native of Ireland, I am a lover of England, and a believer in the necessity of a firm and lasting union between the two countries. Nobody more deeply deplores the disunion at present so apparent between them. For the objects, and still more for the methods of the so-called 'dynamite party,' I have the deepest abhorrence. Is it necessary to point out to any candid reader how widely different is the employment of dynamite in open war from its use as the instrument of secret murder and assassination, and of the destruction of public monuments which are a heritage and possession, not of the English people alone, but of all mankind?

The incidents of this story are purely imaginary; but the ideas and forces with which it deals are real, and may at any moment be brought into active play by the inevitable development of the 're- sources of civilisation.' Such development is certain to take place; it is in rapid progress at this moment. It may not take the precise form indicated in the following pages; but that is a matter of secondary importance. Come it will in some form as little expected, as impos- sible to control. My earnest prayer is that England may be able calmly to await it, clad in the impenetrable mail of Justice and of Right, and strong in the love and devotion of a free and united people.

T. G.

1885.

CONTENTS.

CHAPTER VI.

CHAPTER VII.

CHAPTER VIII.

CHAPTER IX.

CHAPTER X.

CHAPTER XI.

CHAPTER XII.

CHAPTER XIII.

CHAPTER XIV.

CHAPTER XV.

CHAPTER XVI.

CHAPTER XVII.

CHAPTER XVIII.

CHAPTER XIX.

A MODERN DÆDALUS.

INTRODUCTION.

IN submitting to the public the following history of the invention with which my name has been so prominently associated, it is no part of my intention to describe it in scientific terms, or to give any clue to the mechanical principles involved in it. Those, grand and simple as they are, must for the present remain my own exclusive property. When the history of the reception which was accorded to it has been truly recounted, it will be seen that the world has little claim on my confidence or gratitude. My immediate aim in writing is to give such a narrative. So many versions of the story are afloat that I owe it to myself, if not to the public, to state the plain truth, and to show by doing so, who are chiefly to blame for the unexpected and lamentable series of occurrences which immediately followed my first attempt to give a new power to man, and extend his empire over the material world. For those occurrences I have no wish to disclaim whatever share of responsibility may fairly rest upon me; but I shall show that I was obliged to deal with men who, by acting only from a selfish and short-sighted regard to their own exclusive interests, proved that they were not to be moved, except by an appeal to their equally selfish fears.

In truth, the possessor of such a secret is armed by it with a power which in some degree explains, if it does not excuse, the treatment I received from the country I sought to serve.

A man who has solved so successfully as I have done the problem of aerial flight, wields an instrument which, while it may make him a most valuable servant of the State, may at any moment convert him into a most formidable enemy. Would it not therefore be wise to to secure his friendship and co-operation on any terms, unless prepared to extinguish at once himself and his invention, and with them all chance of realising what has from the earliest ages been one of the main objects of human hope and effort? It would not have been hard to make me a friend ; that I was already. All I desired was liberty to pursue my work in peace and quiet, at my own expense and risk ; all I asked was that protection for which the meanest citizen has a right to look. It was refused ; and the State, so far from protecting or assisting, became my chief persecutor and the main obstacle in my path.

This did not happen in the so-called dark

ages of superstitious ignorance, but in the last quarter of the nineteenth century, in the full blaze of scientific illumination, and in the very heyday of mechanical progress. I have spent the best years of my life in unremitting pursuit of one of the oldest and most legitimate of human objects, the study of the conditions of flight, and the construction of flying machines. One by one I have overcome mechanical difficulties which at first appeared insurmountable ; I have brought to perfection an apparatus in the highest degree simple, portable, and inexpensive. I have put within the reach of every one who will devote to the task of learning to use it half the skill and courage which thousands cheerfully expend in learning the use of the bicycle, the power of rising into the air like a bird, of continuing there for hours without fatigue, of guiding his course in whatever direction he may wish, of travelling with a speed equal to that of the eagle, and far surpassing our swiftest railway trains. The bare enumeration of all the powers I have thus at my command would, a year ago, have seemed more like the visions of a lunatic than the statements of a sane and sober mathematician. But within the last few months all has been accomplished in actual fact; the performances of my machine are now as much matters of history as those of the steam engine, and I can speak of them without the appearance of boasting or self-glorification. It is because their reality has been experimentally proved, and the long-dreamed-of possibility of flight translated into actual reality, that the public mind has been so deeply stirred. I fear it must, however, be admitted that the nature of the experiments, rather than the mere fact of their having taken place, lies at the bottom of the popular excitement; and I publish the following narrative as a vindication of the peculiar method of proof which I was forced by circumstances to adopt.

In order that such a vindication may be effective, it will be necessary to enter into many details not directly connected with the main subject ; but I trust that the keen interest which is still felt in the events which I shall be obliged to narrate, and the fact that, until the present, no authentic account of them has been given to the world, will excuse what might under other circumstances be regarded as unpardonable egotism, and wearisome prolixity.

JOHN O'HALLORAN.

DUBLIN, 30*th February* 1887.

CHAPTER I.

DREAMS AND DREAMERS.

SO early did the idea of rivalling the flight of birds take possession of my mind, and so greatly was it intensified and nurtured by the surroundings amid which my boyhood and youth were spent, that the history of my invention, if traced from its first inception and followed through all the different phases of its development, would be almost a history of my life. Born and brought up in a wild and remote spot on the precipitous coast of the North of Ireland, one of my earliest recollections is of the wonder and interest with which I used to watch for hours the gliding flight of the sea birds which made their homes by millions on the

A

inaccessible cliffs and lonely stacks of that bold
front which the headlands of Donegal present
to the Atlantic waves.   Their easy, graceful
motion—ascending and descending invisible
spiral stairs without a tremor of the wing—had
an irresistible fascination for me.   One of my
earliest efforts in experimental mechanics was
the construction of a kite from the stiffened skin
and wings of a gull which had been shot by my
father. This, by means of an ingenious com-
bination of cords, I was able to control and
guide through the air at the greatest height to
which my ball of twine would reach.   It was
the wonder and envy of my school-fellows, and
many were the attempts made to imitate it ;
but I alone knew the secret of the governing
cords, which with precocious instinct I kept to
myself.

The knack displayed in this and in some
other little inventions attracted the attention of
the master of the village school I attended, himself a man of mechanical tastes, and of some
mathematical ability, and I became from that

time his favourite pupil. A docile and studious lad, without taste for the rude games in which my school-fellows delighted, I profited by his instructions. So enthusiastically did I pursue the study of the fascinating subjects to which he introduced me, that my demand for books soon outran the slender resources of his library ; and my father, with the ambition so characteristic of the Ulster peasant, began to dream of a university career and professional position, to be attained by my own cleverness and industry. I shared his hopes, and applied myself so sedulously to realise them, that when I left my home at the age of sixteen for one of the provincial colleges, it was to obtain with ease an entrance scholarship, and to astonish my professors with the amount of my mathematical knowledge, and the extent and variety of my reading in natural and physical science.

During my career as a student, I easily carried all honours before me, and the prizes and exhibitions that fell to my share enabled me to live independently of my father, and to devote myself

unremittingly to the investigations and experiments in which I delighted. These, however,
proved all too successful and absorbing for the
plans that had been formed for me. At the end
of my university course, I found myself with an
excellent degree indeed, but with the tastes and
habits of a mere student and bookworm; without
any knowledge of the world of men, or any pro-
fession by which I might earn my bread. Indeed the shy and unsocial habits I had formed
would have been an almost insuperable barrier
to my success in any professional career.

This did not for a moment trouble me. I
had already convinced myself of the possibility of flight by mechanical means, and my
ambition was now to work out in material
form what I had already demonstrated on
paper. Instead, therefore, of pursuing my
studies with a view to entering one of the
learned professions, as my father had planned,
or attempting to gain a livelihood by teaching,
as most of my fellow-students did, I disguised
myself in a suit of moleskins, presented myself

before the foreman of the blacksmiths' department of a large iron-foundry, where I obtained
employment, and where for several months I
worked for weekly wages. I was at last
forced to leave by the dislike and jealousy
of the regular workmen, with whom I would
not drink, and who soon discovered I was not
one of themselves. Meantime, I had obtained
what I wanted, a practical knowledge of the
manufacture and tempering of steel, and of the
manipulations of fine metal-work.

In search of the leisure and privacy required to
perfect the apparatus which was now in course
of construction, and for the experimental trials
necessary to ensure success, I now returned to
the remote and lonely dwelling of my father
among the Donegal hills. Here, free from all
interruption and distraction, except the scepti-
cism of my relatives, and the disappointment
with which they regarded a spoilt career and
a lunatic craze, I was permitted to enact the
part of a harmless madman, as they deemed it.

Abstracted and unobservant, however, as I

habitually was, and now a thousand times more than ever, because I found myself on the very point of realising the object to which I had devoted all my powers and sacrificed all my prospects, I could not help perceiving that I was living among dreamers as abstracted as myself; idealists much further removed from what I took to be the hard realities of life; and madmen whose craze, if I could have admitted that it had any reality whatever, I should not assuredly have deemed harmless. I found my home strangely altered on my return to it My mother had died during my absence; but even that was not sufficient to account for the change which had passed over my father and brothers. I had left them cheerful, busy, and contented, diligently cultivating the little holding which the industry of their forefathers had reclaimed from the waste bog and heath of the mountain side, of which they looked forward to becoming the proprietors after a few more years of labour and frugality. I returned to find them gloomy, idle, suspicious, filled with a literature of whose very existence I was previously unaware, but of which they were as keen students as I myself was of mathematical and physical science. The whole history of Russian Nihilism, of German Socialism, of the Italian Carbonari, of the French Commune, was at their fingers' ends, and on the rare occasions on which I formed one of the evening fireside group, I found myself listening to discussions turning upon events of which till then I had been profoundly ignorant, and learnt that we were supposed to be living in the midst of such scenes as I had hitherto fancied could not be nearer in time than the Spanish Conquest of South America, or in space than the Russian prisons in Siberia, which I had always half-believed to be mythical.

In truth the change which I found in them was but a reflex in miniature of that which had passed over many Ulster homes, and the history of one family might almost stand as that of a province in those years. For some time

after the last great and honest attempt of a
British Parliament to place Irish farmers in a
satisfactory position, they had lived in comparative comfort and independence, and had
been able to lay by as a small reserve the
profits of their labour, which had been previously absorbed in the rack-rent levied by
their aristocratic and absentee landlord.   But
now times were changing again.   The great
statesman to whose efforts their emancipation
was mainly due, had been driven from power
by a gust of popular passion, consequent upon
the failure of his Eastern policy.   His successor
belonged to the opposite political party, with
which it was an article of faith that Ireland
only needed 'rest' and the repression of agitation.   He reversed at once the action of the
land-courts, suppressed the 'disloyal' newspapers, and forbade public meetings, filling the
country with police and soldiery, and preserving
a tranquillity to which he triumphantly pointed
as a proof that nothing was needed but the
strong hand.   Rents rose above their old figure,

evictions were of daily occurrence, capital was attracted in abundance, and the Tory millennium of wealthy landlords and a starving peasantry began to be realised. But deep mutterings of discontent filled the country, rising to a sustained scream of indignation in Parliament, where the Irish leader, at the head of a compact brigade of seventy members, revelled in a perfect carnival of obstruction, and for the time united both English parties in stern opposition to any and every Irish demand.

This policy was fast bearing its inevitable fruits. Men hitherto 'loyal' were now to be found in the 'Nationalist' ranks, and the Presbyterian ministers of the North vied as popular leaders with the Catholic priests of the South and West. My father and brothers—staunch supporters of the English connection as long as they hoped for justice at the hands of an English Parliament — now threw themselves with stern energy into the popular movement, and for some months their house had been the scene of secret meetings, and the storehouse for an immense armoury of modern weapons, including dynamite bombs of New York manufacture. Absorbed in wild hopes and enthusiastic dreams of a regenerated Ireland, they looked on me as unpractical and unpatriotic; as wasting in useless and impossible speculations the genius and learning which might have been invaluable to their cause. In truth, I regarded that cause as hopeless; I detested the policy of the party then in power, but I regarded the prospects of a rising as too desperate to be entertained.

CHAPTER II.

MURDER.

IT is impossible to describe the delight, the mental exaltation, and the sense of power that possessed me, as, after hundreds of partially successful trials and of consequent alterations and modifications, the hope and expectation of success gradually rose into assured certainty, and I found myself in possession of a power that increased with every opportunity of practice, until the movements that at first were timid, hesitating, and uncertain, became bold, decided, and almost automatic in their ease and precision. Every fresh trial confirmed the boldness and confidence with which I used the apparatus ; every

difficulty suggested an improvement, and every
improvement carried it more nearly to perfection. Already I was beginning to make
little excursions over the wilder and less
populous parts of the county, to accustom
myself to steer a definite course by the aid of
the compass, and to recognise the various
features of a landscape from a lofty elevation.
The wind, which at first had been my greatest
difficulty, became, as I grew more expert, my
chief aid and assistance ; I longed for a breeze
like a sailor. I found it necessary, however,
to carry weights in a wind ; and nothing
surprised me more than this. At first I had
spent much ingenuity in devising dresses which
might be inflated with hydrogen gas, and so
aid in diminishing the weight to be lifted.
These served me indeed, but it was as corks
serve the swimmer ; as soon as I became accustomed to the element, I cast them aside as
an incumbrance. And—strange paradox !—I
found, as my practice increased, that a certain
amount of ballast gave me a power, a speed,

and an ability to stem and make use of the
winds, that appeared almost unlimited.

Nothing surprised me more on these excursions than the loneliness and desolation of
the wide stretches of country over which I
travelled. Rarely was the smoke of a cabin
seen rising into the air. The cabins themselves
were visible on all sides; but they stood un-
inhabited and roofless, imparting a deeper
solitude to scenes that even in my own memory
had swarmed with life and activity. My
scientific reading had not led me into the
regions of political economy; if it had, I should
probably have consoled myself by reflecting
that the altered aspect of the landscape, so far
from betokening poverty or misery, only showed
the influx of capital, and the conversion of
small holdings into great sheep-farms and deer-
forests. The poverty and misery were to be
found elsewhere; partly in the hamlets that
clustered round the secluded bays on the coast,
where the inhabitants eked out their scanty
harvests by fishing; but principally in the

slums of such great towns as Belfast, Liverpool, and Glasgow, to which they had drifted, to form the lowest, poorest, and most turbulent stratum of the population.

I was no political economist, however, and the sight of roofless cottages where I remembered to have seen happy families; of sheep dotted over lonely hillsides, that I had seen covered with bands of labourers ; of deer wandering through green glens, where I recalled the plough at work, used to fill me with the most unscientific sorrow and indignation. More especially when the cabin stood roofless as the result of a recent eviction ; when, as on one occasion, I actually caught sight of the smoke rising from the still smouldering thatch that had been stripped off by the ' crowbar brigade,' and saw the houseless wretches who had lived under it standing like statues of despair upon the roadside among their broken and worthless furniture; then it must be confessed I lost sight of the fact that these tenants had foolishly contracted to pay a higher rent than the holding was worth, nay, had, in many cases, paid ruinous sums for the 'tenant-right,' and denuded themselves of the capital necessary to carry on any profitable work whatever. And at such times I gave way to feelings unworthy of a philosopher, and cursed the proprietors of the soil in language borrowed from the vocabulary of my brothers, whose expressions usually made up in rude vigour what they lacked in cultured breadth and polish.

Political questions, however, entered little into my thoughts as I went out one day with my completed apparatus strapped up into a neat and portable parcel, and bent my steps to the brow of a lofty cliff that overhung the sea about a mile from our solitary dwelling. From this point I had determined to start upon a longer journey than I had yet attempted, and to put to a severe test the speed and endurance of which I was capable in the air. I had resolved to make in one excursion the circuit of the entire island, which I calculated I should be able to do in six or seven hours. I am speaking of sober facts, but of a kind which were then so extraordinary, and which are still so foreign to the experience of most of my readers, that I do not know how to describe them without appearing to use the language of wild exaggeration. I paused on the brink among the wheeling seagulls, four hundred feet above the waves which broke unheard in long sinuous lines of white among the rocks below. Then I unfolded and strapped to my shoulders a pair of wings, each about six feet long, and without hesitation launched myself into the empty air, in which I floated gently and gradually downwards, varying my course with perfect ease and precision by throwing my weight to one side or the other as I wished to turn. The fresh wind met me as I cleared an angle of the cliff, and setting myself against it, I rose without an effort until I soared far above the rock from which I had sprung, and hung suspended in mid-air,

> ' As if I floated there
> By the sole act of my unlorded will
> Which buoyed me proudly up.'

Proudly indeed! I cannot hope to paint the
pride, the rapture, the triumph which swelled
my heart at the success of my experiment,
the dreams that crowded thick and fast upon
my mind, the hopes that rose within me! Not
dreams of gain, nor hopes of fame, but wonder at the new powers, the fresh sources of
delight, the untrammelled facilities of intercourse that my discovery seemed to promise
to mankind. What additions to the sum of
human pleasure; what an extension of mutual
knowledge and brotherhood among nations;
what new and higher forms of civilisation;
what a revolution in the social and political
conditions of the race seemed now about to be
inaugurated! Before I again touched solid
earth my mind had travelled round the entire
compass of the globe, and my body had made
the circuit of Ireland with a speed that seemed
magical. From a lofty height, at which I must
have seemed a mere floating speck in the sky,
I followed the windings of a coast spread like
a coloured chart below me. The historic towers

of Londonderry, the picturesque shores of Magilligan and Portrush, the beetling precipices of Fair Head, dwarfed into flatness by the height from which I viewed them, passed under me like the gliding of a river; the wild coast of Antrim, the cloud of smoke that hid Belfast, the fertile fields of Down and Meath and Dublin, the lovely hills and glens of Wicklow, the rich vales of Waterford and Cork, the gleaming lakes of Kerry, the broad estuary of the Shannon, the towering cliffs of Clare, the island-studded waters of Galway and Mayo, chased each other beneath me like figures in a dream — such a panorama as scarce another land could show! The broad midsummer sun went down in a crimson glow behind the Atlantic wave, and the full moon lifted itself slowly above the broad shoulder of Errigal as I descended towards the earth again in the uncertain twilight to study from a more familiar elevation, the landmarks of my course; for I was now returning to my starting-point, after such an excursion as had never been taken by man before, unless the story of Dædalus be true.

The moon was now shining with a broad and brilliant lustre that showed every stone and tuft of bracken on the lighted side of the hills with the clearness of noonday, while on the other side everything was lost in deep impenetrable shadow. Below me stretched a long white winding line, here extending bare and straight across an open space of moorland, there plunging into the gloom of a deep wooded glen, again appearing to skirt the curving shore of some deeply indented bay, further on zigzagging up or down the slope of some hill which, flat enough when viewed from my elevation, was still a very steep reality to the horse or man obliged to toil step by step over it; for I was looking down upon the highroad connecting the scattered villages and dwellings of that part of the county with each other and with the outside world.

Not a single habitation was visible, and hardly a sign of life, except a black object that seemed

to crawl at a snail's pace along the road below.
It gave me an exulting sense of power to note
the exceeding slowness of its progress, for
although it hardly seemed to move I knew
well it was a light dog-cart drawn by the
swiftest horse in the county, and driven by the
smartest whip in Ulster—no other than ' Tom
Crawford,' the sporting agent to Lord ——,
known over all the country as the quickest
shot, the keenest rider, the most merciless
tyrant, and the jolliest good fellow to be found
for fifty miles. I was not near enough to see
the details of the picture, but I knew that of
the two men in the trap one was the agent,
and that in each of his side pockets was a
loaded revolver. I knew that the man seated
beside him was a sergeant of police, and that
he held a Winchester repeating rifle between
his knees; that the dark speck a hundred
yards in front was a mounted policeman, and
that another followed at an equal distance
behind. I knew moreover that they were returning from an eviction ; that ten miles behind

them they had left a dozen roofless cabins, from which they had ejected fifty starving creatures, whose only offence was inability to pay their rents and live on their little potato patches; that aged and bedridden men and women and helpless children were sleeping that night on the roadside and among the heather, and that to-morrow they would be trying to make their way to the nearest workhouse. Remember that I was the son of an Irish peasant farmer, himself liable to the same treatment at any moment, and do not blame me that my heart swelled within me with bitter hatred and indignation. 'Before heaven,' I muttered to myself, 'if I saw the rifles levelled at this moment which were to cut short their accursed lives, I would not stoop to utter a single word of warning!'

Even as I looked, lo, it happened! Not on the roadside or behind the dry stone fences, to which the stupid policemen devoted their attention, but far out on the moor, on an elevated knoll which commanded a long stretch of the

road, the gleam of polished metal caught my
eye. Here, concealed by a few bushes of gorse
from the observation of their victims, but
plainly visible from above, two men lay on
their backs, the barrels of their Metford rifles
resting across their toes, and coolly covered
the advancing group as deliberately as if shooting off the last tie at Creedmoor or Wimbledon.
One fierce flash streamed out, and long before
the scarcely audible crack which followed it
had reached my ears, I saw the agent spring
from his seat, throw up his arms, and tumble
over the wheel into the road, where he lay
motionless.

For a moment the man who had fired turned
on his face and peered through the furze-bush
which concealed him, using a binocular field-
glass to make sure that the right man had
fallen. The other remained in the attitude in
which I had first seen him, till they were apparently satisfied that there was no necessity
for a second shot. Then they both crawled on
hands and knees among the bracken, never

once rising to their feet, until they reached
the edge of a steep declivity, down which they
plunged into a wooded glen and were lost to
my sight.

Meanwhile, the policemen, who thought of
nothing but the fences and ditches on the
immediate roadside, seemed quite at a loss to
imagine whence the fatal shot had come. They
galloped back and forward along the road,
and then began to scour the moor, until one
of their horses fell into a deep turf cutting,
from which his rider extricated him with some
difficulty.

Do not suppose that I wasted much time in
watching their proceedings. The moment I
saw that the drama was over, that the agent
was dead, and that his slayer had made good
his escape, I bethought me of my own safety.
I did not feel called upon to give any information, with the certainty of having to ex-
plain the very peculiar circumstances under
which I had witnessed the crime, to an in-
credulous judge and a probably hostile jury.

Swiftly as the previous part of my journey had been accomplished, the last ten miles was the best part of the record. In little more than five minutes I alighted in front of my father's cottage.

CHAPTER III.

'KILLING NO MURDER.'

WHEN I entered my father's house late on that eventful night, but still in time for our frugal supper of porridge —or, as we called it, stirabout—and milk, I was asked no questions. The vagaries of so eccentric and unaccountable a person had long ago ceased to have any interest for my father and brothers, wrapped up as they were in the prosecution of their own dark and dangerous designs. My father had long since told me that, as I had received a liberal education, and would not labour on the farm like my brothers, I must not expect to share any profits that might be made from it. My brothers regarded

me as an idle and useless interloper, too dainty
to soil my hands with ordinary farm work, and
too spiritless to join in striking a blow against
the gentry, with whom they fancied I classed
myself, because of my superior education.
There was no sympathy and little intercourse
between us, and no curiosity or interest re-
garding my movements was ever expressed.
Had my mother been living it might have
been different ; but since her death, my position
in the family had been rather that of a tolerated
intruder, than of a son and brother.

To-night, however, I was filled with triumph ;
I had at last vindicated the usefulness of the
pursuit in which I had been so long absorbed ;
I felt a strange and rapturous elation that
lifted me above the barrier of silence usually
interposed between myself and them, and a
sense of independence in the possession of so
extraordinary a power. I burned, moreover,
to speak of the tragedy I had just witnessed,
and to plead with them against that course of
secret agitation in which they were engaged,

which could only lead to crime and disaster,
and still deeper misery to the unhappy country
they sought to serve. As we sat down to table,
I hardly noticed that Dan, my eldest brother,
was absent; that was not so unusual as to
form any subject of remark. The rest were
evidently in an excited and abstracted state,
and in no mood to be interested in any concern
of mine.

'Father,' I broke out, ' I tried my machine
to-day, and I have succeeded beyond my
wildest hopes. I can fly like any bird. I knew
I should be able to do it, but I never hoped
for anything so good as the reality.'

'How often have you told us that before,
my lad?' responded my father incredulously.
'Don't talk to me about flying; I'm sick of
the very name of it! Even if you have
been able to flutter down from the roof of
a shed without breaking your bones, what's
the use of it, or the sense of it! I wish to
heaven you would give up such foolish non-
sense, and turn to something that would make

you bread and butter ! It is not much longer you will be able to get them here ; we can't live with our present rents, God help us ! and things are getting worse and worse. It's the tenants of Ballybunnion are being turned out of house and home this day, and it will be our turn next, if Tom Crawford has his way much longer.'

'You needn't trouble yourself about Tom Crawford, father,' said I ; 'he'll strip the thatch off no more cabins. He is lying dead on the Ballybunnion road, a mile beyond Widow Armour's corner.

A quick glance passed between my father and the other three.

'Where's Dan, boys ?' he asked, hurriedly. 'And how do you know anything about Tom Crawford ? It's a good twenty miles from here to Widow Armour's corner, by the road, and the agent wouldn't be further than that by this hour.'

'You seem to know his movements pretty well,' I answered ; 'it is not more than twenty minutes since he reached the turn of the road, and there he was killed by a single rifle shot, fired from the knoll on the moor, at a range of five hundred yards. It was a shot that might have won the Queen's prize at Wimbledon, and it was enough, for not another was fired.'

'And the man—the man who fired it—what of him? did he get away? was he taken?' he demanded, in wild excitement, without once seeming to notice the apparent impossibility of my knowing anything about it. 'Well done! well done! cool heart and steady hand! I warrant he never left trail that any policeman could follow. Tell me again, boy, tell me again! Only one shot! Did the cowardly peelers never pull a trigger?'

'Father!' said I, deeply shocked and horrified, 'you don't surely approve of such doings? You don't think a cowardly murder ever served any cause, or ever will?'

'Murder!' he answered, sternly; 'who talks of murder? Put the saddle on the right horse, boy. Was it murder to turn old Biddy

Macarthy at eighty out on the roadside, where she died within a week ? Was it murder to turn out Pat Heraghty's wife, with her baby a day old, to tramp twenty miles through the snow to Letterkenny last Christmas, and to drop with cold and hunger on the road ? Call such things as that by their right name, and that's murder ; but when the murderer gets the bullet he deserves, it's God's justice, if it isn't man's.'

'It's just such talk, and such doings, have kept us down, and will keep us down till the end of time. You unite both parties in England against you by your unreasoning violence, while the only hope you have is in the hearty support of one of them.'

'Hear the philosopher !' exclaimed Dick, my second brother. 'He has read English history till he thinks no other nation under heaven has the right to be free, or the power to enforce it. But we know a little too, though we haven't been to college, and we can tell him there has been a Washington as well as a Hampden, and a Garibaldi as well as a Gladstone.'

'Right, Dick,' I rejoined, 'I'm with you there ; but when did Washington or Garibaldi advocate murder or assassination ?'

'If they didn't advocate it with pen or tongue they acted it with musket and bayonet at Bunker Hill and Palermo—such murder as we do here. It's all one. They leave us no other way.'

'Suppose the English take you at your word —as they will some day — and lynch every Irishman in London? You'll find it is not so pleasant to be at war, when it is not all on one side.'

'Pleasant! have they made it pleasant for us? Go to Ballybunnion and see! They have had it all their own way long enough; but we'll show them something of the other side of it before long. The Boers taught us a lesson at Majuba Hill that hasn't been thrown away, and there are a thousand lads in Ireland who could hit an officer between the eyes at a thousand yards, and never throw away an ounce of lead. You saw a specimen of our marksmen to-night—if you *did* see him. But I don't believe you did ; how could you tell what happened ten miles off only half-an-hour ago, unless you were able to be in two places at once, like Sir Boyle Roach's bird ? '

'Well, believe me or not, just as you please —I told you before I could fly like a bird, and you never paid any heed to it. I was having a little excursion round the country, and happened to see what I saw. But of course it is of no consequence to you. Good-night, father ; I feel a little tired after it, and I am off to bed.'

'Hold on, my lad !' exclaimed my father, awaking from a reverie in which he had been plunged, 'what about this machine? Have you really made anything of it? were you really able to travel ten miles in as many minutes? for that, and no less, you must have done if the agent was shot to-night at the turn of the road, and you were there to see it.'

'Yes, father,' I answered, proudly, 'I have done all I say, and more. I have worked out an invention which will make all our fortunes, while you thought I was only idling. I can't tell you what I have done; you wouldn't believe it! I have travelled a thousand miles with it this day since noon! but you couldn't imagine what it is unless you saw it.'

'Travelled a thousand miles! but come— seeing is believing, and this is past believing unless you see it. Where are the wings? I'm a fool even to think it—and yet if you saw what you say—but come, let us settle this at once.'

We all followed him out to the little garden in front of the house, where I produced the wings, and strapped them on amid the breathless expectation of the whole group. I then leaped lightly on the low wall, sprang into the air, and with a few strokes floated over their heads. Then rapidly mounting, I made a wide sweep high over the tops of the trees that closed around in a dark semi-circle. The moon,

C

though low in the west, was still bright enough to show my movements distinctly.

When I alighted they were speechless with astonishment. Everything else was forgotten for the moment, and as soon as the boys found their tongues, they were clamorous for a trial of their own powers there and then. I now found how much the use of the apparatus depended upon the skill and practice of the user. My own mind had dwelt so long upon the method to be pursued, that when the moment of trial came, I almost instinctively adopted the right position, and threw myself upon the empty air with the confidence which was absolutely necessary to success. But none of them had the slightest previous idea of the principles or forces to which they were to trust, and the result was as futile and ludicrous as the first efforts of a beginner to learn the use of the bicycle. A few feeble and ungraceful flutterings, utterly ineffective for any purpose of locomotion, were all that any of them could achieve. It was plain that much practice would be necessary before the art could be acquired, and that many might be constitutionally unable ever to acquire it. At last they desisted from their efforts, and we stood talking in the waning moonlight, too excited to think of sleep, and full of the most extravagant hopes and fancies. I found myself for the first time a hero among them, the acknowledged genius of the family, instead of the useless dreamer. Even my father forgot his usual sternness, and the gloom which had for years been habitual with him was chased from his brow and tone.

'I have done you injustice, Jack,' he said, laying his hand kindly on my shoulder. 'I did think you were wasting your talents and education. I did think you were forgetting the wrongs and sorrows of your country, and throwing away the power and opportunity to serve her, in selfish and useless indolence. I see I was mistaken; you have beaten us all; you have done more than the whole of us put together. This will ensure the triumph of Old Ireland. You must keep it a secret; you must set yourself to train your brothers and other young men, till we have a flying brigade that can go anywhere and do anything! Nothing will be able to stand against it, and you will have the glory of delivering your country and striking the chains from her hands! Oh! Jack, I am a proud man to see this day!'

'Oh, father,' I answered, 'how can I make the first use of my discovery in causing war and bloodshed? It is not for war, it is for peace! it is not for one people only, it is for all the world! I would rather bury it in the sea than that one life should be sacrificed, much less a bloody war provoked.'

'You talk like a silly girl,' said he. 'Don't you see there is war already, and it's sure to last all the longer because we are so weak and so few in comparison with the enemy. But give us a weapon like this, and we will soon put an end to it! and then there will be no more evictions, lad; no toilers starving to fatten idlers and profligates; no need to strike down the oppressor and the bloodsucker, and take the precious lives you are so tender over, as if it were not a good deed to rid the world of them. Peace and brotherhood indeed! peace with robbers, and brotherhood with murderers! No, boy! the only way is to exterminate them from the face of the earth, and then there will be peace worth talking about.'

'Never will I join in such a mad and hopeless and wicked enterprise!' I rejoined hotly. 'I don't believe that men are parcelled out into tribes and nations, one all good and the other all bad. It is by drawing out the good in all, and not by setting one against another, that anything can be done.'

'Rubbish!' he answered, angrily; 'do you think you are in a debating club? we are practical men, and we know the worth of such talk. I did think once that freedom was to be won by great speeches and fine sentiments, but you can see what came of trusting to that! Freedom never lasts unless it is clamped with iron and cemented with blood, and one ounce of lead weighs heavier than fifty columns of speeches. But I'm a fool to be talking myself. If you hesitate to serve your country in her hour of need, you are no son of mine. Only I will take care that you do not do her any injury.'

'You need not fear my doing her any injury,' said I; 'God knows, I love her too well, and feel her sorrows too deeply! But oh, father, think what an injury you may do her without meaning it, if you plunge her into a conflict with an enemy that is too strong for her, and if you stain her hands with midnight murder and assassination. It is only the old hopeless story; an hour of wild revenge followed by a century of legalised injustice. For God's sake, think better of it, and take what has come to us as a means by which we may rise out of our poverty by honest work, not as a fresh occasion for plotting and violence that can only sink us deeper in the end! Think of all we may do for our country in a peaceful way, with the wealth and power that this discovery will bring us.'

'We'll think of that after the wrong is
righted,' said he, 'but we must shake the
chains off our hands before we can do free
work with them. That's the first thing to be
done, and the man who thinks of anything
else is a slave, and deserves to remain one!'

CHAPTER IV.

BANISHED.

THE moon had set while we stood talking, and the chill breath of morning began to shiver among the leaves of the trees that still surrounded the house with an impenetrable wall of darkness. As I sadly folded up and strapped together the apparatus I had unfurled so proudly an hour before, we heard the little gate open and shut, quick footsteps sounded on 'the gravelled pathway, and the next moment my brother Dan stood among us. Pale, weary, and covered with mud and earth-stains, he had a light in his eye that the darkness could not hide. In his hand he carried a long and handsomely-mounted rifle

which he carefully placed against the wall.
'Rest there, my dark Rosaleen,' he said, tenderly patting the barrel, 'you have done good work to-night. Father, were you watching for me? There is no need for anything more to-night. Rosaleen did the trick beautifully; five hundred yards, and the police never thought of looking further than the points of their noses, as if she were a horse-pistol or a blunderbuss! Ah, they have to reckon with a different sort of weapon now, and different eyes behind them.'

'Hush!' said Dick, with a meaning glance towards me.

'Who—what?' cried Dan, with a quick look round. 'Ah—it's only Jack—I forgot he knew nothing. Never mind, he's not going to inform; he'll forget all about it when he begins to his models and fal-lals again. Hey Jack, how go the wings? have you flown over the moon yet, my budding angel?'

'Don't speak to me!—don't come near me!' I almost shrieked, in the first horror of standing face to face with a manslayer. 'I saw you do

it, and your hand is red with blood !' Here he
held up both hands and glanced quickly at
them. 'Ay, you may well look, your soul is
red with it! I won't tell, but I won't speak to
you—I won't sleep under the roof with you!
Away, away!'

'What has come to the boy?' said he, con-
temptuously. 'Who told him anything? you
might have known better than trust a secret to
a screeching idiot like that. Hark you, my
lad! it's nothing to me what you think or what
you know, but you had better put a stopper on
your tongue, and a tight one, or I'll do it for
you in a way you won't like! A country's
cause is not to be risked because a chicken-
hearted boy turns sick at the colour of blood.'

'Don't provoke him, Dan,' said my father;
'he may help us yet, when he gets over his
squeamishness, and makes up his mind to be a
man and a patriot, as he will before long. I
have good reason for what I say, which I will
tell you presently. But we must go in now,
and get a little sleep before morning; it would

not do to have any difference noticed by anyone who may happen around. Come in, boys ;
come, Jack ; you must be one of us now, and
we will soon teach you to sing a more manly
tune.'

I stood hesitating in the chill morning air
after the others had gone in, a hundred con-
flicting impulses surging wildly in my mind.
With all the horror I felt at the sudden reve-
lation of crime and violence, I could not help
a certain sympathy and admiration mingling.
How cool and determined they all were ! how
free from womanish curiosity and personal fear,
and all doubt of the righteousness of their
cause ! And was it not a righteous cause ?
How often had my own blood boiled at the
scenes I saw or heard of almost daily ? how
often had the exclamation, ' They deserve to
be shot !' sprung to my lips ! And here I was
shrinking like a woman from what I had over
and over again declared and believed to be an
act of justice ! Could it be that I was really
chicken-hearted ? What a man of iron Dan

was! with what magnificent steadiness and
nerve he had fired the avenging shot, and how
cool and unflurried he was through it all, and
after a midnight run across ten miles of bog
and mountain! I felt sure he would sleep as
soundly as a child that night. And I knew
that if he had to answer for his deed with his
life he would never blench, but would walk to
his death with an unfaltering step, and with the
prayer, 'God save Ireland!' on his lips. Was
there not grandeur in the devotion with which
he was risking life and soul for his native land?
And I might do the same! I might bring
them aid which even he could not afford, and
which would lead to almost certain victory. I
turned almost dizzy as the thought rushed in
upon my brain, now first realised in its full
force and meaning.

My father's voice broke in upon the tumult
of my thoughts.

'Come in, Jack,' he said, calmly, 'and get to
bed ; no quarrelling with your brothers, for we
shall all have to hold together like steel. Re-

member, my boy, you are an Irishman too, and
your country needs you all. Give me that parcel; I will put it up till to-morrow. And then
you shall know all about our plans, and make
up your mind what you will do.'

I surrendered my parcel without a word, and
followed him into the house. Upon a settle in
the kitchen Dan was stretched, already un-
dressed and sound asleep. Every line of his
bold and handsome face, every curve of his tall
and athletic figure, spoke of repose and peace,
and his breathing was soft and regular as an
infant's.

'There is a son to be proud of!' said my
father, gazing fondly on the sleeping giant.
'Brave as a lion; steady as a rock; true as
tempered steel! I am proud of you too, Jack.
I never knew you till to-night, and I see you
have genius; you will bring us brains, which
are worth more than muscle. I thought you a
boy; you will show yourself a man. Not a
word; we will talk to-morrow; to sleep now.
Good-night.'

I felt that I, too, had never known him before, and began for the first time to see what
had made this man a leader among his fellows·
His mingled sternness and tenderness subdued
and attracted me; I felt I should have a hard
task to resist his iron will. But as I turned
away from Dan I shuddered in spite of the
unwilling admiration I was compelled to feel,
and could not have forced myself to touch him
had a kingdom depended upon it. I climbed
up a narrow stair to the attic where my younger
brothers were already asleep, and lay down.
On every side the calm regular breathing of
the unconscious sleepers came to my ears, while
I, the only one among them on whose head no
blood lay, tossed and turned on my unquiet
pillow as if the guilt were mine, and mine alone.
A thousand times the pale and ghastly figure
of the murdered agent rose before me, and I
was compelled to picture again and again the
scene that must have passed when the body
was brought home to his wife and children.
In vain I struggled to master my thoughts and

reduce them to control; to ask myself rationally whether such things were not inevitable in every struggle for freedom; whether it was anything more than a just retribution for inhuman cruelty; whether I might not righteously take part in such a conflict? The hopelessness of it, the utter wickedness of it, the betrayal of the highest interests of humanity it would involve, kept beating in upon my brain like the refrain of an endless song, and I found it utterly impossible to frame a rational thought upon the subject. The whole thing was so foreign to my settled habits of thought, so revolting to every ideal I had ever formed, that I could not force myself to think calmly of it. It was long after daylight had streamed into the apartment that I fell into the dreamless sleep of utter exhaustion, from which I did not awake until my usual hour for rising was long past.

On going down I found my father alone. My brothers had long before finished their breakfast, and were engaged in their usual day's labour, just as if the occurrences of the day before had been matters of the most ordinary routine. I ate my late breakfast almost in silence, striving to brace up my resolution for the struggle which I knew was at hand, in which I felt by no means assured of victory.

'I have not disturbed you this morning, Jack,' said my father at length, 'because you had a rather exhausting day yesterday, and I wish you to lend all the vigour of your mind to what I am going to say. This invention of yours will greatly advance matters. We can now look forward with hope to the issue of a conflict, for it will increase our strength a hundred-fold, and make a hundred men more than a match for ten thousand. It alters the aspect of the question entirely.'

'Do you mean,' I asked, 'that it will make an armed rising possible which would not be thought of without it.'

'Exactly,' said he. 'It must come sooner or later. But although many things are ready; although there are at this moment some thousands of men drilled and armed, and ready to respond to the call of their leaders, yet they are too few, and those leaders have not judged it wise to precipitate a conflict with the forces at their disposal. But this changes everything, and gives us an advantage which will sweep all before it.'

'Then,' said I, 'if it depends on me to make such a rising possible, I will never do it. It would be a mad and criminal act to endeavour to gain by murder and bloodshed what we might get by peaceable means.'

'We shall never get it by peaceable means. If people had always submitted tamely to oppression, as you would have us do, there would never have been freedom of any kind, and the most glorious pages of history would never have been written. Bloodshed! you are greatly afraid of bloodshed. Nothing great was ever done without it; and the man who shrinks either from taking life or losing it for his country, is a worthless poltroon.'

'Then O'Connell was a worthless poltroon,

D

and Isaac Butt was a worthless poltroon, and so have been the best men of all ages and countries. Besides, I don't hate the English ; I love and admire them. I would rather by far be a part of the great British Empire, than a fifth-rate little Irish Republic, if we could be even that. I hate their present Government, but not the nation itself ; it is the greatest nation under heaven, and the freest.'

'I will waste no more words with you,' said he, rising in bitter wrath. 'The friend and admirer of my country's greatest enemies can be no friend of mine. Go, boy, from the home you have disgraced and the land you have betrayed, and let me forget that I ever had such a worthless son.'

'I have disgraced no home, and betrayed no country,' said I. 'You had better keep such words for the murderer of Tom Crawford, instead of the only one of your sons who is free from his blood. Give me my machine, and let me go. It will at least keep me from starving.'

'Ay—you will sell it to the English Government, will you, and make your fortune out of the ruin of your country? No; I am not going to give you the means of committing such an infamy. If it is not to be used for Ireland, it shall be destroyed.'

'Who talks of infamy?' I answered, passionately. 'Will you add robbery to murder? Will you steal my brains from me, because I will not help you to do murder wholesale, and then talk to me of infamy?'

'I will take very good care you do not give any advantage to the enemy beyond what they possess already. You shall not take a stick or a stone away with you, beyond the clothes on your back. As for your machine, I will keep it safe. It may be someone will be found who will be able to use it as well as you, and it would be a pity to throw even such a chance away. Now take yourself out of my sight, and never let me see your face again, unless it be to tell me you have changed your mind, and determined to do your duty to Ireland and to me.'

'I will not go,' I said, 'without what rightfully belongs to me. You have no right to keep it from me, and I will have it before I leave the house.'

He stepped to the door and blew a loud whistle on his fingers, to which there was an immediate reply, and presently my four brothers came running in from the farmyard. Dan took in the situation at a glance, as he looked at the group we presented before the door ; the old man with upraised hand and glittering eye, his grey hair streaming wildly over his flushed and swollen forehead ; I, with eyes also flashing with suppressed fire, and an unwonted look of determination on my face.

'So,' he said, 'he refuses, does he ? Didn't I tell you he was English at heart? the spawn of those cursed Government colleges always are.'

'I have sent him about his business,' said my father ; 'there is no room for traitors here.'

'Are you mad, father?' said Dick; 'he will go straight to London and sell his invention to the English Government.'

'Ah, I'll take care of that; I have it under lock and key. And if he goes to London, he'll have to beg his way. He sha'n't have a penny from me.'

'But don't you see he has it in his head all the time,' rejoined Dick. 'He'll easily make a new one in London, and then we shall be worse off than ever.'

'How can we help it, short of keeping him a close prisoner, or silencing him altogether? The first we could never do; the last is not to be thought of, for he is our own flesh and blood after all. But he must swear a solemn oath before he goes, that he will have no dealings with the Government.'

'You may make your minds easy on that score,' said I. 'Badly as you have treated me, and wicked as I believe your objects to be, I have no thought of doing anything to your injury. No, Dan, not even of telling the police who shot Tom Crawford, though I'm sure there will be a handsome reward offered for the information. I swear solemnly I will do nothing against Ireland; I am no enemy, though not a friend in your sense. Now I'm off; good-bye,' and only waiting to get my hat, I turned away, and walked off, leaving the group standing before the house. Something was shouted after me, and I heard a smart altercation going on among them; but I paid no heed, and walked swiftly down the glen leading to the highroad. In truth, I was in fear of being detained by force; and it was not until I reached the public road, and had passed a number of habitations, that I ceased to dread pursuit, and to look more frequently back than forward.

I was bending my steps towards Letterkenny, which was distant about twenty miles. It was the nearest town of any importance, but I selected it as my destination mainly because it was the residence of two gentlemen who had formerly been my fellow-students, and with whom I had kept up some degree of intimacy after leaving college. One of them was now Coroner for that division of the county, the other an Inspector of National Schools. My plans were simple. I intended to see one or both of them, to interest them in my invention, and ask their assistance in getting it brought before the public, in which, if I succeeded, I had no doubt I should soon be able to repay them amply.

CHAPTER V.

FRIENDS.

THE afternoon was well advanced when I entered Letterkenny, weary and footsore, feeling how different was the mode of locomotion to which I was obliged to resort, from that which I could have employed if I had not been robbed of my invention. The first thing that caught my eye was a freshly printed police placard offering a reward for any information respecting the murder of Mr Crawford. I found the town full of rumours and surmises on the subject, but there appeared to be no suspicion of the truth. Some Americans had been observed to embark hurriedly on the Allan Co.'s steamer at Moville in the morning, and the popular theory placed the murderer among them.

On inquiring for my friend the Coroner, I found he was just then absent, making arrangements for the inquest, which was to be held on the following day. I need hardly say I did not apply to be examined as a witness. I next bent my steps to the lodgings of the Inspector, who was at home, and received me heartily.

I unfolded the circumstances under which I had made my visit, explaining that I had left my father's house on account of a family quarrel. And here I found my first difficulty ; for not having my machine at hand to prove my assertion that I had really mastered the art of flying, I found my friend not unnaturally sceptical of the reality of my invention. He was sufficiently well acquainted with mathematical physics to be aware of the enormous antecedent improbability of such an invention having been made, and it was plain that he regarded me as being under a delusion on the subject.

'My dear fellow,' he explained, as we sat over a glass of whisky punch after dinner, 'the thing is absolutely impossible. I remember a man at college in our time who thought he had done it. And he certainly had devised a machine, working by a set of vanes, and attached to a reservoir of hydrogen gas, which would lift the weight of his body into the air. It was worked by electricity. But it would only go for a very limited time, and it was quite incapable of making way against a very moderate wind; even a four-mile breeze it could not face. It stands to reason; for look at the almost infinitesimally small co-efficient of resistance of the air, and you will see that, to make anything of it, either an extent of surface is required that is quite incompatible with lightness, or a quickness of stroke that no mechanism can give. You will find, however well you may think it looks on paper, that it won't work when you come to try it. If anything at all can be said to be mathematically and experimentally demonstrated, the impossibility of mechanical flight is that very thing.'

'On the contrary,' said I, 'its possibility is demonstrated by every sparrow that flies across the road. The very same atmospheric and mechanical difficulties exist in the case of the sparrow, and it is for man to find out how they are overcome, and apply the same principles to his own case. That is what I have done. That it has never been done before, is no proof of its impossibility. And I am quite prepared to give you an experimental proof whose force you cannot resist, by flying bodily over the tops of these houses before your eyes, as soon as I have completed a new machine.'

My friend good-humouredly shook his head, and it was quite plain he had a doubt of my perfect sanity. He invited me, however, to remain with him for such time as might be necessary to construct another apparatus, engaging, if that should prove as successful as I expected, to give me any further assistance that might be required. And so I took up my quarters with him for the time. The very modest stock of money I had brought with me was expended in the purchase of tools and materials. I set up a little workshop in an unused shed behind the house in which he lodged, and for two or three weeks spent almost every hour of daylight in incessant work.

I saw very little of my other friend, the Coroner, whose duties were heavy just then. After a long period of enforced tranquillity— perhaps in consequence of it—the epidemic of agrarian murder had broken out again. No sooner had a verdict of 'wilful murder by some person or persons unknown' been returned in the case of Mr Crawford, than three landlords were shot in rapid succession in different parts of the county. All were killed in the same way—by rifle shots from a distance so great that the assassins invariably succeeded in escaping without even being seen; and it became evident that there was a gang of skilful marksmen at work. In one case only

was any clue discovered—a rifle which had
evidently been abandoned in the hurry of
escape. It was a small-bore muzzle-loading
match rifle of the most modern make, furnished with patent wind-guage, telescopic
sights, micrometer screws, and 'all the latest
improvements.' But although a most valuable
and costly weapon, the police were quite unable to find an owner for it.

'I declare, Jack,' said the Coroner, one night
as he sat with us at a quiet little supper, 'I
would give you a hundred pounds if you had
that machine of yours finished. Our mounted
police are no use scouring round the country.
What is wanted is someone who could take in
a radius of a couple of miles at a glance. If
you had been the escort on that night Tom
Crawford was shot, we might have had the
murderer at once, and the other men would be
alive at this minute.'

'And the "Crowner" would have been less
rich and less famous than he is, and less puzzled
into the bargain! But seriously, Bob, have you

no notion whatever as to who are at the bottom of this?   Do you think the people of the county have anything to do with it? or is it the work of outsiders and strangers?'

'Nine people out of ten would tell you it must be done by Americans, and I should be inclined to think so myself if I did not remember the "Invincibles." I have no doubt there is a strong American element, as there has been in all recent Irish agitation; but I have just as little that the men who fired the shots are Irishmen, and are probably going out and in among us every day.   No one who does not know them well can have the least idea what a power of dissimulation and concealment the Irish have.   I might have done it myself, and you could never tell.'

'They must be first-rate marksmen, though,' said the Inspector.   'Where will you find fellows among the peasantry who could make a bull's-eye at a thousand yards?   It isn't part of their school training, I can tell you.'

'I rather think it will be found to be all the

work of one or two crack shots among them,'
returned the Coroner. 'Yet it is astonishing
how many of them have learned to shoot, and
shoot well. I have heard it quite openly said,
that if ever there is a rising which has to be put
down by an army, it will be found that there
are a number of first-rate shots told off for the
purpose of shooting the officers. Without any
reflection on the courage of the British army,
I think that would be found rather trying.'

'I call that low,' said the Inspector.

'It is very effective, though,' said I, 'as was
shown in the Boer war. It may be very fine to
look on war as a game among gentlemen, to be
carried on with a chivalrous regard for the feelings of an opponent; but democracies will
regard it as a hateful necessity, to be gone
through in grim earnest, and brought to an
end as soon as possible by real, downright
blows with the sharpest weapons that can be
found.'

'Well,' said the Coroner, as he rose to leave,
'there is a reward of one thousand pounds

already offered by the Government to anyone who will help them to lay their hands on any of the murderers. You might do worse than take to watching the county, if you get your machine perfected. And it will probably be ten thousand pounds before long, if many more are shot in the same way, without its being found out who did it.'

'Thank you,' I replied, 'I don't quite relish the idea of being a target to one of these sharp-shooters. I have no doubt they would be quite equal to a flying shot ; and the game would be all in their favour, for they would have plenty of cover, and I could have none.'

In spite, however, of all the vigilance and activity of the police, and of the fact of a great Government reward being offered, the murders remained as great a mystery as ever, and from time to time more were added to the list, while public excitement in England rose to fever heat, and fresh 'coercion bills' were pressed through Parliament in hot haste, only to fail of their effect. That basis of public support was gone

without which no law can have any real force.
Again and again the Irish leader was challenged
to disavow sympathy with the advanced wing
of the Nationalists ; again and again he coldly
declined to answer questions which were insults,
and asked whether there was anything surprising in the fact that desperate oppression was
producing desperate crime. More than once he
had been mobbed in the streets, and half his
followers were in a state of chronic suspension.
Public business was almost at a deadlock, and
the extreme tension, it was evident, could not
last much longer.

But the daily business of life goes on with
very little change amid the gravest and most
exciting political complications ; and, keenly
interested as I was in the situation of public
affairs, I would hardly spare the time even for
a glance at the morning newspaper, so absorbed
was I in completing the machine on which I
was engaged. After about three weeks of incessant toil it was ready for trial. My two
friends, who had taken the greatest interest in

E

every step, and had been more than half convinced by the explanations I had freely made to
them, were almost as much excited as myself.

In the early dawn of a clear summer morning
we met by previous appointment, and proceeded
to the large empty yard in which I had my
workshop. A minute sufficed for my preparations, which consisted simply in strapping to my
shoulders a light apparatus, the principal part
of which was a huge pair of wings, formed of
stout canvas extended upon light steel rods,
and I stood before them in a form almost
exactly resembling that which the popular
mythology attributes to angels.

'Success to you!' shouted the Coroner, as
I sprang upwards. I had never doubted of it,
and I was delighted to find that my new
machine worked even better than the first. I
made a wide sweep over the tops of the houses,
circled round the town, still silent and sleeping,
and returned to the spot where my two friends
were standing transfixed with astonishment.
Their enthusiasm knew no bounds, and they

hurrahed and clapped their hands like school-
boys. Then each would have a trial for himself; but although I explained the method of
using it, which seemed so natural and easy to
myself, neither of them could succeed in catch-
ing it at the first attempt. Fearing to injure
the apparatus, they desisted.

'You shall each have one, the very first I make,'
I cried, 'for you have helped me generously.
I hope the Commissioners won't cut off your
travelling allowances, Mr Inspector, for this will
supersede both horse and railway, and will cost
you nothing to keep.'

'I'll wait till I can manage it better,' said he,
'or I should soon be a case for our friend the
Crowner. I can't imagine how you do it. It
seems to me to give no lifting power whatever.'

'No more could I imagine,' said I, 'the first
time I saw a bicycle, how it was kept upright
without falling; or the first time I found myself
in deep water without corks, how I was to keep
afloat. I had far more trouble in learning to
swim than in learning to fly.'

'Come in now to breakfast,' said our host. 'I have ordered it early this morning, as I have to visit a school almost on the border of my district. It will take us within an easy drive of Strabane, and you can just take the car on for so far, if you must leave us in such a hurry as you say. You will easily catch the mid-day train to Belfast.'

'Train me no trains,' said I ; 'do you think I would stoop to travel by such antiquated contrivances as steam-engines or railroads, or crawl along at thirty miles an hour when I can easily do a hundred ? No, sir! I am going to advertise myself in a more effective style than that. Who would believe I could fly through the air if I took to the train when I wanted to travel? You little think what a revolution I am going to inaugurate this day.'

'And do you really mean to fly all the way to London ?' he asked, in astonishment. 'How long do you expect to be on the way ? '

'I can do, I believe, about a hundred miles an hour. London is about four hundred miles from here. If I start at 10 A.M., then I shall arrive at 2 or 2.30 P.M.—just as the people who left Belfast at 8 last night are getting into Euston.'

' Have you ever been there before ; and how will you find the way ? '

' I was there once, in my student days,' I said ; ' and as for finding the way, I have little fear of that. I have a pocket compass, and shall keep a general south-eastern direction. Even if I miss it I shall hit the coast beyond, and it will be easy to find from any part of Kent or Essex. It will only be an hour or two more.'

' One would fancy we were in the " Arabian Nights," or that Munchausen had come to life again. I can hardly believe even yet that what I saw this morning was true.'

A few slight preparations were all I had to make. My friends pressed upon me the loan of a small sum for immediate expenses, jestingly saying they knew they were making an excellent investment. Then, after many farewells and hearty wishes for good luck, I equipped myself for my journey. I had no luggage to carry, and even the small sandwich case and wine flask I placed in my pocket appeared a superfluity. I started from the doorstep in full view of about a dozen persons who were in the street at the time, and from the look of petrified amazement which was the last thing I observed as my two friends stood waving their hands to me, I had no doubt they would be closely besieged with questions for the proverbial nine days.

CHAPTER VI.

LONDON ASTONISHED.

P, up, and still upwards in the fresh morning air I held my course, until a vast apparent concavity lay below me, partially hidden by patches of cloud, which looked like lakes and seas of mist clinging to the surface of the ground. As I went on they became more frequent and dense, until they spread like an unbroken ocean beneath me, the snow-white surface heaved into great rolling billows, over which my shadow flitted up and down, the only moving thing visible in the vast and weird solitude. Below the cloud-floor, it was probably raining heavily; above, the naked sun beat down fiercely on the snowy masses beneath, until the

unbroken glare of light was almost more than
I could bear.   Even in that keen blaze of
sunshine the cold was intense, and I resolved
that my next excursion should be made in
winter clothing, of which I now felt the
want greatly.   After I had travelled about
an hour in a south-east direction, I observed
the clouds in front begin to break up into
masses ; a wind sprung up from the south-west,
and the temperature at once rose several degrees,
a change I welcomed gladly, for I was becoming
benumbed with cold.   The clouds, no longer
forming an unbroken floor beneath me, were now
piled up in vast and mountainous masses, amid
which I threaded my way in such a dream of
admiration and amazement as cannot be expressed in words.   The stupendous grandeur of
these cloud-landscapes, the towering heights, the
yawning rifts, the fathomless abysses they disclosed, were such as no terrestrial Alps could
rival.   Sometimes their great swelling domes
and sheer precipices looked solid as the snowy
peak of Chimborazo ; but again the shifting out-

lines and the indescribable play of light and colour in their translucent masses belied the impression of mountain strength and fastness. Amid deep-cloven ravines and overhanging cliffs of vapour I steered a devious course, avoiding the phantom capes and promontories as if they had been solid rock ; for although I knew I could plunge at will into their misty substance, an overpowering sense of awe, almost of terror, at the weird, gigantic forms around me, had crept upon my mind, and I dared not violate their secrets.

Far below, through many a rift and chasm, I could see the green and laughing surface of the earth, the blue and sparkling sea ; and I plunged downwards to be nearer it, for it felt homelike after the awful solitude and silence of the middle cloud region. I was now leaving the land behind, and about to cross the Irish Channel. The sea spread blue and clear in front, its surface flecked with white, for a brisk south-west breeze was blowing. On this I was swept rapidly out to sea. In an incredibly short time the mountainous coast of Westmoreland appeared in sight, and, steering like an eagle to the top of the 'Black Coombe,' I alighted, and folded my wings for a few minutes' rest and refreshment.

Up and away again, this time bearing more directly south. The few minutes' contact with mother earth had renewed my courage. I now plunged without fear into the substance of the clouds, and found it exceedingly like mere terrestrial mist. But it blinded and confused me, and I found it better to avoid it if possible. Flying at a moderate height, I had a bird's-eye view of the country beneath. I could see towns, farmhouses, roads, railways. Upon these last were always visible trains, conspicuous by the long white trail of steam ; and I found that I could always outstrip their speed with ease.

London at last! for surely that great dim cloud of smoke covering several degrees of the horizon could be nothing else ! How was I to approach it? where take up my quarters? I remembered a quiet little hotel in one of the streets leading from the Thames Embankment

to the Strand, and there I determined to lodge
for the present. But first I intended to create
a little sensation.

Coming in from the west, I flew low, scarcely
more than clearing the tops of the houses, and
I could see that my course was being watched
by many in the streets below. The open space
of Hyde Park soon came into view, and I
alighted for a moment on the bridge over the
Serpentine. Seeing several people running
towards me, I rose again, kept my way slowly
down Piccadilly, St James' Street, Pall Mall,
and so to Trafalgar Square, where I made two
or three circles in the air, and finally alighted
on the top of Nelson's Monument. The hero's
cocked hat afforded ample room to sit and
survey the scene beneath. I could see crowds
of people running from the west and entering
the square, where they stood gazing upwards,
while the hum of their voices rose louder and
louder as their numbers increased. Soon a
surging multitude filled the square, and I felt
that it was time to gratify their curiosity still

further.   Leaving my lofty perch, I sailed
slowly round two or three times, amid a perfect
roar of excitement from the assembled crowd.
I had intended to alight upon one of the lions
at the base of the monument; but they were
already covered with spectators anxious to
secure the most commanding points of view.
Finding it impossible to alight anywhere, and
fearing to trust myself among the crowd, I
rose again, and held my way southward, towards the Abbey and St Stephen's.   But now
the crowd poured in a solid mass down Whitehall, and I heard shouts and screams, not all of
wonder or amazement, but of anger and of
terror as well.   Realising the danger of the
charge of such a dense mob down a crowded
thoroughfare, I suddenly changed my course,
quickened my speed, and shot over the tops of
the houses in an eastward direction, never
stopping until I reached St Paul's, where I
alighted upon the little gilded gallery below
the ball.

From this point of vantage I could look down

Ludgate Hill and up Fleet Street. All seemed quiet as usual. Down below I could see half-a-dozen people looking upwards and pointing to me. But presently I descried the symptoms of a 'block' in Fleet Street. Cabs and omnibuses were jammed together in an inextricable mass, and the energetic blasphemy of their drivers rose high above the usual hum of the streets. A surging tide of humanity came first trickling and then bursting through; the mob rushed up Ludgate Hill in twos and threes, in dozens, in scores, in hundreds, and soon every part of St Paul's Churchyard which I could see was occupied by a shouting, struggling, swaying mass of people, their faces all turned upwards, and every finger pointing where I stood.

For a minute I stood dazed and uncertain what to do next; this was more than I had calculated on. The mere force and weight of the mob amazed and alarmed me, and I thought with horror of what must have happened in the crowded streets along which they had heed-lessly rushed. I was in no mood to favour them with another exhibition, although, from the wild shouts below, I could guess they were demanding one. My chief wish now was to escape from them, and lay the devil I had unintentionally raised.

I rapidly strove to recall the exact locality of the hotel I had determined to stay in, which was in one of the small streets off the Thames Embankment. Then I rose again, amid a hoarse yell from the crowd below, made two or three wide spiral sweeps to gain a lofty elevation, and suddenly shot downwards like a stooping hawk towards a spot on the Embankment near the Temple pier. Fortunately the place was entirely deserted at that hour. Here I found a secluded nook at the foot of Essex Street, where I hastily unstrapped my wings and folded them up. Then, with a neat parcel, like a tourist's 'hold-all,' of brown waterproof canvas in my hand, I walked down the Embankment towards Westminster, turned into a quiet street in the Adelphi, and presented myself at the door of one of the private hotels with which that region abounds. Here I engaged a room, and ordered a quiet tea and chop to be ready in an hour.

CHAPTER VII.

GOING TO PRESS.

AVING secured a resting-place and possible retreat, I now strolled into the streets, and, turning down the Strand, took my way towards St Paul's. The great crowd that had gathered there seemed to have broken up, and to be streaming towards Westminster, with an idea that the object of their curiosity would be found in that direction. As the different groups elbowed their way past me in the Strand, I caught many fragments of description, and many conjectures as to the course I had taken. It appeared to be the one absorbing topic of conversation. But it was clear that I had successfully evaded pursuit. Of the hundreds who passed me in the street, not one had the slightest idea that the quiet-looking youth whom he rudely pushed aside was the very person of whose exploits he was at that moment talking at the pitch of his voice, and at whose whereabouts he was confidently guessing.

'*Globe* or *Echo*, sir! last edition! full description of the flying man!! sixteen people trampled to death in the streets!!! great dynamite plot to blow up St Paul's!!!!'

It was the voice of a newsboy, loaded with papers hardly yet dry from the press. So great was the demand that I could hardly fight my way through the crowd in time to secure almost the last copy of each paper. I retreated into a by-street to glance at them, and was relieved to find that the boy had been drawing on his imagination for some of his facts. No lives had actually been lost, though several accidents were reported. But the inventive genius of the writers had no difficulty in discovering the motive that had prompted me.

F

Undoubtedly it was part of a dynamite conspiracy, and the police were at that moment on the roof of St Paul's, searching for the infernal machine I had been seen to carry there.

As I stood laughing quietly at the credulity of mankind, I observed that I was close to the *Echo* office. A crowd of boys was pouring past me, loaded with a fresh edition. A sudden thought occurred to me, and I walked in and asked to see the editor on important business.

'He's too busy; no one can see him that he doesn't know,' said the clerk to whom I spoke.

'Tell him,' said I, 'that I can give him special information about this business, and if he won't have it, I will go to the *Globe.*'

'Come with me then,' said he, and I followed him to the editor's sanctum, where he sat busily writing.

'Well—anything fresh?' he asked, looking up.

'Here's a man who has information about the plot,' said the clerk, shutting me into the room.

'What can you tell me, and who is your authority?' asked the editor briefly.

'I am my own authority,' said I. 'I happen to know all about this matter, and if you give me a hundred pounds, I will write you a column giving a true statement of the facts.'

'That's a cool proposal,' said he.

'It will be worth three times as much to you, and if you don't accept the offer, I will make it to the *Globe* for two hundred. Take it or not as you please.'

'How am I to know you are not an impostor?'

'If you give me your word to keep the secret,' I returned, 'I will give you conclusive proof that I am the man who flew over the city to-day. You can have it by taking five minutes' drive in a hansom.'

'I give you my word, then, that if you prove that, I will keep the secret, and pay you well besides. Come along quickly.'

As he spoke, he somewhat ostentatiously transferred a small revolver from a drawer in the desk to his pocket, seized his hat, and jumped up to go.

We drove rapidly through the crowded street to my hotel, where I took him upstairs to my room. I unfolded the wings, and showed them to him.

'That is all the proof I can give you,' I said, 'for I only came to town a couple of hours ago, and I have no friends or acquaintances. But it ought to be enough.'

'It is enough,' he answered. 'Now let us get back as quickly as possible. I say nothing,' he continued, as we drove rapidly back, 'about the risk you may be running in making your affairs public. That's your own look-out. I simply pay you for early and authentic intelligence. If it compromise you or anyone else, you must take care of yourself.'

'If you think there is any plot in the matter,' said I, 'you are mistaken, that's all. It is purely a private enterprise of my own, and no one else has any connection with it whatever.'

'Here are a pen and ink, here are slips of paper, and here is a cheque for one hundred pounds,' said he, as we sat down again in the office. 'The devil will call for copy in five minutes, and every five minutes till you have done. It takes about a dozen slips to make a column. Now, fire away, and let's get the edition out by six o'clock.'

I began by flatly contradicting all the rumours of a plot that were afloat. Then I gave a short popular sketch of my invention, withholding, however, my name and country. I described my arrival in London, and the incidents which followed, concealing my present address. In conclusion, I stated that I appeared merely as an inventor, and that I intended to make and sell machines similar to that which had become so famous, and to teach their use. Almost as fast as the slips were written they were carried off, and within an hour of the time I had first entered the office, the new edition was being sold by thousands of copies.

The editor rubbed his hands and chuckled gleefully. 'It's the best stroke we have done for a long time,' said he; 'come and have a chop with me, and then we'll go down to the

House, where you may expect to hear yourself denounced as a public enemy, and me as a credulous fool for not seeing at a glance what a villain and impostor you are.'

CHAPTER VIII.

A DEBATE IN THE HOUSE.

THE House was just filling up after the dinner-hour as we pressed our way through the densely-crowded passages and lobbies, through which the police with difficulty kept open lanes for the members to pass. 'Wait further back, gentlemen, please. Beg pardon, sir, you can't pass here. It's no use, sir; gallery's quite full.' My conductor, like many press men, was himself a member. He whispered a few words to the official, who at once removed his arm and allowed me to pass into the inner lobby. Here I looked around with keen interest, for among the groups of legislators standing round in earnest conversation, I recognised many a face which the photographer's art, or the cartoons of *Punch*, had made familiar to all the world.

In another minute I found myself seated in a little box beneath the gallery, separated only by a cross-bar from the members of the House. I was at first surprised at the emptiness of the House itself, compared with the crowded and animated condition of the lobbies outside. A member was on his legs making a speech, while the few who were scattered up and down the benches conversed in low tones, or buried themselves in papers, or seemed to slumber, and appeared to pay no attention whatever to what was being said. After a short time, however, the aspect of the chamber began to change. The benches gradually filled up, and there was quite an animated hum of conversation. Presently an hon. member 'below the gangway' rose to ask permission to put a question to the Secretary of State for Home Affairs.

It was rather informal, he said, but perhaps the extraordinary nature of the circumstances under which he rose, would justify a departure from the usual practice. There had occurred that afternoon an event of an unprecedented nature. It was reported that a man had actually been seen to fly over a considerable part of the city. He had been seen to alight on the roof of St Paul's Cathedral, and to deposit there something which it was feared might be an explosive of a destructive nature. The popular apprehension connected the occurrence with what was known as the 'party of action' among Irish Nationalists, and, in the present highly excited state of popular feeling, there was some danger that such ideas might lead to rioting and violence, from which loyal and peaceably disposed Irishmen would be the first to suffer. He wished to know if Her Majesty's Government had any information to lay before the House of a nature calculated to allay such apprehensions.

The Home Secretary said that his noble friend appeared to him to have missed the essential point in the remarkable occurrence which had been reported, and to have fastened his

attention upon what was accidental and infer-
ential. There appeared to be no doubt that
the extraordinary feat of flying through the air
had been successfully performed. That, in the
opinion of Her Majesty's Government, was a
fact not only of great public interest, but of
immense political importance. As to its immediate connection, however, with any existing political organisation, they had absolutely
no evidence whatever. The police had been
directed to search the roof of St Paul's, but
nothing had been discovered of an explosive or
dangerous nature. He recommended his noble
friend to restrain his own flights of fancy, which
were more likely than anything else to bring
about the danger he deprecated on behalf of
certain estimable and law-abiding classes in the
community.

The noble lord begged to say, in reply, that
if the members of Her Majesty's Government
would themselves condescend to what had been
called the scientific use of the imagination, they
could not fail to see in the occurrence of that

afternoon a new and terrible danger to the
State. It was all very well for them to say
that there was no evidence before them ; but
were they going to wait until our public buildings
were flying about our ears, before they would
see what was evident to everybody else ? It was
not to be wondered at that the public mind was
very deeply stirred and disturbed, for what
vigilance would suffice to guard against an
enemy who could transport himself at will
through the air, and evade the most watchful
sentinels? He did not wonder that the popular instinct, which was always a more reliable
guide than the theories of philosophers or the
shifty explanations of politicians, connected this
incident with the machinations of that party
from whose ingenuity the country had already
suffered so much. For his part, he trembled to
think what might be the consequence, in the
present excited state of public feeling, to that
large section of the population who, although
hailing from a sister island, were nevertheless
loyal and law-abiding. He thought every one

of them owed it to himself to separate himself clearly from every possible suspicion. He appealed to the leader of the Irish party, whom he saw in his place, to disavow, on behalf of himself, his colleagues, and his country, all sympathy and complicity in any such designs as the public, however mistakenly, were only too ready to suspect.

There were loud cries for the Irish leader, but he kept his seat, looking around with a very perceptible sneer upon his finely-cut features. One of his lieutenants, however, sprang to his feet as the previous speaker concluded.

Was it any wonder, he demanded, that Irishmen were not in love with the Parliament in which such a scene as this was possible? in which the most insulting insinuations that a perverted ingenuity could devise were daily based upon occurrences as innocent as that which at present engaged their attention? He for one was not going to make any such disavowal as had been demanded. On the contrary, he rejoiced in the brilliant discovery that had been made, and he only hoped it was true that it was the invention of an Irishman. What a position were their opponents in, by their own showing! Conscious that they were acting in defiance of all reason, of all civilisation, of all that was right and natural in human feeling, they found themselves compelled to dread every step in advance, to look upon every scientific invention as the work of an enemy, to attempt to stifle everything that would extend communication and cement the bonds of brotherhood among men. They felt as if by instinct that anything which had the effect of elevating and educating men must work to their disadvantage. For his part, he gloried in the progress of the race, for progress must lead to freedom ; and if this grand discovery could be made to lead to the freedom of Ireland, he gloried in it all the more. He could not express his contempt for the cowardice that could see in it only a fresh source of danger, and the malignity that could only make a fresh opportunity of slandering and discrediting political opponents out of an event

at which every honest man ought to re-
joice.

Here was a proof, rejoined a member from the
opposite side, if any proof were wanted, of the
feelings with which a certain number of hon.
members regarded anything that was likely to
constitute a danger to the State. Instead of
honourably and straightforwardly disassociating
himself from the dangerous designs and criminal
hopes known to be entertained in may quarters,
the hon. member hastened to announce his sympathy and admiration, and to express his hopes
that this terrible weapon might be of some use
to those who were labouring for the disintegra-
tion of the Empire and the disruption of Society!
Did the follower speak with the sanction of the
leader, and was the latter at last going to give
an authoritative endorsement, by his silence, to
the grave suspicions which that speech was
calculated to arouse? If so, he feared the most
lamentable consequences were likely to ensue,
and he warned the hon. gentleman that silence
would not lessen the responsibility that would

rest upon him if, for want of a few reassuring
words, he allowed the impression to remain that
Irishmen generally were willing to condone
violence and outrage if it only led to the loss of
English lives and the weakening of English
power.

Still the Irish chief sat sneering and silent,
amid the din of cheers and counter cheers which
greeted the close of every speech. Presently
there was a lull, as the Home Secretary was
seen standing at the table with a copy of the
Echo in his hand.

'Perhaps it will calm the excited minds of
some hon. members,' he said, 'and convince the
noble lord who raised the discussion, that Her
Majesty's Government are not the political idiots
he courteously assumes them to be, if I read to
the House some passages of an article written,
I am informed, by the inventor of this flying
machine, and published in a late edition of one
of the evening papers.' He proceeded to read
the article I had written a few hours before.
'It will now appear,' he added, 'that Her

Majesty's Government are neither fools nor madmen when they say they have no evidence of any dangerous design on the part of this individual, who, on the contrary, appears to be well-disposed, and only anxious to serve his country by introducing a new industry and fresh facilities for locomotion.'

' Will the Right Hon. gentleman further inform the House of the name of this patriotic and philanthropic individual ? ' asked the member who had first spoken.

' He withholds his name, as he is quite entitled to do,' said the Home Secretary. ' That is a matter of no public concern.'

' And his nationality ? ' persisted his questioner ; ' does he conceal that as well as his name ? and will the Right Hon. gentleman tell us that is a matter of no public interest either ? '

' Not the slightest,' said the Home Secretary. ' I must protest, in the name of Her Majesty's Government, against the waste of time involved in such frivolous questions and irregular discussions as the present. There is absolutely nothing to be gained by them, and I must decline to answer any more questions on the subject.'

'Since the Right Hon. gentleman is determined to burke further discussion on a matter of such momentous and pressing importance,' returned the other, 'I have no option, Mr Speaker, in the discharge of a public duty, except to move the adjournment of the House.'

'Has the noble lord forty members to support his proposal?' demanded the Speaker.

A great number rose to their feet, and it being evident there were more than forty, the orator proceeded.

It was with the greatest reluctance that he took this course, but the unaccountable slowness of Ministers to perceive what was obvious to the meanest capacity, and the extraordinary credulity with which they accepted what was, after all, a very transparent attempt to lead them astray, left him no alternative except to take this somewhat irregular method of arousing them to a sense of the necessity of vigilance in times of such imminent public peril as the pres-

G

ent, or, failing in that, to sound that note of warning to the country which its official sentinels were too much wrapped in blind security to give. No one could help being touched by the childlike innocence and faith with which the Home Secretary accepted the assurance of an anonymous writer that a certain unknown person had no connection with that party of crime and outrage which was known to exist, and whose favourite methods were strikingly in harmony with the disclosures that had been made that day. But such faith and confidence, however touching and beautiful in a child, were only ludicrous in a grown-up man, and became almost criminal in a responsible official entrusted with the guardianship of the lives and property of his countrymen. What was the ground of the Right Hon. gentleman's confidence? He was almost ashamed of having to point out how very flimsy and worthless it was. It was simply an article in an evening paper, by a writer who withheld his name, who concealed his nationality, and whose identity with the inventor

of the machine rested only on his own assertion—the assertion of a man who was afraid to
let his name and country be known, or to lay
public claim to an invention which, if honestly
made, must cover its author with fame and fill
his pockets with gold ! Was it possible, was
it credible, that any man who had made such
a brilliant, such an important invention, would
hesitate to come forward and claim the reward
of his abilities, unless he were conscious of
motives and designs that would not bear investigation ? And yet it was on the mere word of
such a man that the Home Secretary bade them
close their eyes in calm security, and lull all
their fears to rest ! How did he know that the
writer and the inventor were one and the same
person ? Everybody knew how eager these
evening papers were for startling news, and
what was easier than for some clever impostor
to step forward and assume the character of the
unknown person of whom everybody was talking
for the moment ? He got his price for his article,
the public palate was tickled with a new sensa-

tion, the paper had an increased sale, and everyone was satisfied, while the country was deceived.
Nay more, what would be easier than to disarm
public suspicion, and lead away investigation on
a false scent by such means, especially when a
gullible Home Secretary could be found to assure
the country that all was innocent and harmless ?
He confessed that he shuddered to think of the
possible dangers into which a too easy-going
and credulous Ministry were leading their trusting countrymen ; but even as of old, when the
guardian dogs of the Capitol slumbered, the
cackling of the geese gave warning of the treach-
erous onslaught of the enemy : so he trusted
that the voice of even so humble and perhaps
foolish an individual as himself might arouse
the country to a sense of its danger ere it were
too late.   The quarter from which an attack
might be expected was only too well known.
There was even in that House, in the very citadel
of the constitution, a party whose avowed object
was to break it up ; a party who devoted all
their energies to the task of embarrassing the

House and obstructing public business; a party
who, he would not say challenged, but implored
to speak a word in condemnation of such crimes
and outrages as had unhappily been too frequent, had persistently refused, and one of whose
spokesmen they had heard that night openly
rejoicing in the new engine of warfare that
had been introduced on the scene. Let the
country be on its guard against a danger so
well known and so thoroughly understood ;
and if Ministers were too blind or too supine to
provide promptly for the safety of the State, let
the people themselves take measures to exact
those guarantees of loyalty and good faith which
had not been forthcoming in response to manly
and straightforward appeal. As for this inventor who is so studious to conceal his name and
his nationality and his ulterior designs, let the
Home Secretary prove his intimate knowledge
of him by producing him before them, and giving
them some security that if his talents are not to
be devoted to the service of England, at least
they shall not be used to her injury. He

begged to move the adjournment of the House.

The speaker sat down amid a storm of sounds from all sides of the House, the hearty cheers from his immediate neighbourhood being echoed by the derisive 'Yah! yah!' of the other side. A sudden hush fell upon the chamber as it was perceived that the Irish leader was upon his legs. A bitter smile curled his lip as he looked around, his voice was quiet and incisive, and his manner in striking contrast to the heated declamation of the previous speaker.

'If he were England's greatest enemy,' he said, 'he could never desire to see a more pleasing spectacle than the House just then presented. The day had been one that would live in history, for it had seen the realisation of one of the oldest dreams of humanity. Some unknown man of genius—he knew not who or whence he was, but, like his hon. friend near him, he would be proud if it should appear he was an Irishman—had solved the problem of centuries, had given new powers to man, and

had made that day an epoch in the history of
the race. It was an occasion on which one
would think that political strife might be forgotten, and men of all parties, and of all nations,
unite in recognising a great advance in science
and in civilisation, and in paying a tribute to
the transcendent abilities which had made it
possible. Such, one would think, would be the
duty and the delight of the Representative
Assembly of the British Empire on such an
occasion. Could anything be more humiliat-
ing than the spectacle they actually presented ?
A great and powerful political party, thinking
of nothing else than how they could further
insult, and torture, and goad to madness that
unhappy country which their oppression had
provoked into lamentable crime, and ready for
that object to cast all truth, and candour, and
justice to the winds! a Government bearded
by their own followers, apologising with bated
breath for the existence of the greatest inventor of modern ages, timidly explaining that
they knew no harm of this man, that they had

no evidence that he belonged to the hated and justly-suspected race! They did not know his name? Well, he could assure them that it would be known to posterity when many that he could mention should be quite forgotten. How unutterably paltry and contemptible the little tricks and dodges, the wily turns and subtle manœuvres, in which the lives of parliamentary leaders were passed appeared when compared with the lofty themes which engaged the man of science in his unselfish and beneficent labours for mankind! The spectacle of a British Parliament listening with patience to a proposal that a great invention should be suppressed unless its author would bind himself to their chariot wheels, and give up to party what was meant for mankind, was one of the most shameful that could be imagined; and England's bitterest foe could desire no greater triumph than it afforded. This the bulwark of Freedom, and the Mother of Representative Institutions! It represented England's selfishness and tyranny, and cynical disregard of all interests but her own. Let all the world look on, and realise what a blessing and what a privilege it was to live under a rule so beneficent, so unselfish, so tender of individual rights, so helpful to the general progress of mankind!'

Only a few cheers from his immediate neighbours greeted the conclusion of this speech ; but a hurricane of applause broke forth as a rough and stalwart figure rose from the front opposition bench, and eyed his opponent for a moment like a gladiator before he began.

'Never,' he declared, ' had he listened to a more disappointing, he might say a more heart-breaking speech than had just been addressed to the House. The hon. gentleman had had a great opportunity of reassuring the House, of setting himself right with the country, but it had been lost, and, he feared, lost for ever. He, and the party with whom he had the honour to act, had hoped, in spite of frequent disappointments, that the cloud of suspicion which the proceedings of some of the more violent members of the party led by the hon. member had brought upon the whole of it, would be dispelled by a few frank and manly words; but they had hoped in vain. Why should those words, which would be welcomed by every man on that side of the House, which would strike their sharpest weapon from the hands of the party opposite, remain unspoken? He feared the country would give its own answer to the question; he feared the hon. member had himself supplied materials for an answer. Why need he go out of his way to hold up the Parliament of Great Britain to contempt, in a carefully-considered speech, every sentence of which was brimful of the bitterest sarcasm and the most rancorous hostility? He had no fear that that great assembly would suffer from the sneers of the hon. member; but he could tell them who would suffer. The party he led would suffer; the country he professed to love would suffer; and the interests of peace and civilisation, about which he was so anxious, would suffer most of all.'

The Chancellor of the Exchequer now rose to state the position of the Government.

'It was all very well,' he said, 'for irresponsible and somewhat juvenile orators below the gangway to clamour for strong measures, and to pose as the saviours of the country from imaginary dangers; but if the noble lord ever experienced the responsibility of office, he would find that it would not do to legislate in advance of the necessities of the case, or to propose measures of coercion upon inadequate grounds. He must repeat the statement of his Right Hon. friend, that there was absolutely no evidence connecting the remarkable occurrence of the day with the deplorable crimes and outrages of which they had heard so much. The measures of precaution that had recently been passed, and the extraordinary powers with which the Government had been armed, were quite sufficient to enable them to interpose with effect should any such connection become hereafter manifest, and to cope effectively with any danger that might arise. As for the inventor of the machine of which mention had been made, they had for so far no reason to doubt his good faith. It would be a question with the Government how far it was consistent with the interests of the country —which of course were their supreme guide— to permit the introduction and general use of a means of locomotion which might supersede and render obsolete and valueless communications, internal and external, upon which enormous sums of money had been spent, and in which an immense proportion of national and private wealth had been invested. The question of the increased facility of intercourse with foreign countries was also one which would demand their earnest consideration, especially in view of questions of national defence and military strategy. They could assure the House that they should not be found wanting in regard to such interests, either public or private, as were in danger of being affected ; and that in the future, as in the past, the safety and honour of the State should be their first and last consideration.'

CHAPTER IX.

PUBLIC OPINION.

WHEN the Minister sat down there was a general exodus from the House, the incident being for the time at an end. In a few minutes the member who had introduced me looked in and tapped me on the arm.

'There is nothing of any interest to keep us here any longer,' said he. 'If you have no objection, I should like to introduce you to the Home Secretary, who has expressed a strong desire to see you. Of course, if you wish to remain unknown, I will say nothing more about you; I merely told him I believed I could bring about an interview, if you were willing. He belongs to the opposite party from me, but you will find him an honourable and straightforward. man, and you need not fear being compromised in any way.

'I do not fear it,' said I. 'I have nothing to conceal. I am only sorry I did not sign my name to that article; if I had known how my silence would be misrepresented, I would have left them no handle.'

We passed through what appeared to me an interminable labyrinth of corridors and passages, and presently entered a small and plainly-furnished room, in which the Home Secretary was seated.

'I am happy to make your acquaintance,' he said, shaking my hand cordially, 'and congratulate you on having made a very remarkable invention. I need hardly say, after what passed in the debate at which I understand you were present, that the Government are fully alive to its importance.'

'I am very much flattered,' said I, 'to be the object of so much attention. It was not my intention to trouble the Government in any way about it, further than by asking them for the protection usually accorded to inventors.'

'Ah,' said he, ' most inventions—I may say almost all—are of interest merely to certain trades and industries ; but this is one of very unusual—in fact, national — importance. We shall not fail to evince our sense of its supreme value and significance, once we are satisfied that it is really effective. We will give you every facility for proving that. The members of the Cabinet would be very glad of an opportunity of seeing it in action in some suitable place— say at Woolwich or Chatham.'

'I thank them,' I answered. 'I hope to prove its value to all the world ; indeed, I think I may claim to have done so already. I intend to leave no doubt on the mind of anybody whatever, and shall be delighted to give a demonstration to any number of gentlemen who may wish to witness one.'

'We will understand, then, that you will meet us to-morrow, at a time and place with which I

will acquaint you in the morning. May I in-
quire your address?' I gave it. 'Thank you. I
have further to request that you will keep this
appointment strictly private, and come by the
usual means of travelling. We do not want
such a crowd as your new mode would probably
attract.'

'Publicity is my aim and object, Mr Secretary,'
said I. 'Surely the Government can appoint
a place where they are in no danger of being
annoyed by a crowd?'

'Nevertheless,' said he, 'we shall be obliged
if you will humour us in this matter. May we
consider it settled? Thank you. Now I will
wish you good night,' and with another shake
of the hand I found myself bowed out.

'I congratulate you on your diplomacy,' said
my friend the editor, as he guided me back
through the puzzling maze of passages. 'But
you are hardly old enough for the Home Secretary yet. You were quite right not to commit
yourself to privacy, except as a matter of courtesy; but you will find that Governments give

a wide interpretation to such understandings. However, I have no right to advise, and I see you have not a bad notion of taking care of yourself. Now, good night ; I wouldn't walk home by the Embankment, if I were you. Hope to see you to-morrow; perhaps there will be matter for another article.'

I strolled slowly home by the Embankment, notwithstanding my friend's caution, which I did not understand. The cool night air was grateful after the heated atmosphere of the House, and the wide stretches of the calmly flowing river, glittering with the long lines of light reflected from the electric lamps on bank and bridge, presented a scene of fairy-like beauty and enchantment. I walked on in a sort of dream, from which I was rudely awakened by the rough jostling of a group of young fellows who were passing. I tried to avoid them by stepping aside, but one of them seized my arms from behind, while another knocked my hat over my eyes. I felt hands thrust into my pockets, and groping for my watch chain. As I kicked

H

and struggled, too much taken by surprise to think of calling out, I saw a man emerge from the shadow of a bridge behind, and run towards us. Immediately, although my assailants were at least half-a-dozen, they let go their hold and ran off in different directions.

'A bad lot, sir,' said the man. 'See if your watch and money are safe. It was very foolish of you to come here alone at this hour, but I guess you are a stranger.'

'It was lucky you were so near,' said I, when I had satisfied myself I had lost nothing. 'But what about yourself? Didn't I see you in Palace Yard five minutes ago?'

'I am on my way home, sir; but it's different with me; it's easy to see I wouldn't be worth the trouble of robbing. A gentleman like you is another matter. May I see you to your door, sir? for it's desperately unsafe of nights along here.'

A few steps more brought me to my lodgings, where I dismissed my conductor with half-a-crown. It was still early, but I felt weary, and had no wish to go out again. I sat for a while in the coffee-room listening to the conversation of two or three loungers over the report of the debate in one of the evening papers.

' A rattling good speech I call that of Lord ——'s,' said one. ' The Government are all very well, but they want keeping up to the mark, and he's the boy to do it.'

' Did you ever hear anything so venomous as the Irishmen's speeches, especially the last?' said another. ' But F— showed them up finely. Why on earth those fellows won't say a word against the outrages I can't imagine, unless they sympathise with them, as it is quite clear they do.'

' Would you believe they were sincere if they did?' asked another. ' You know very well, and they know it too, that you have made up your mind they are mixed up with them, and you would only say they were hypocrites if they said a word to the contrary.'

' Let me tell you, though,' said a fourth, ' that P— knows very well what he is about. That speech of his is by far the ablest in the debate.

It was not a reply to Lord ⸺ ; it was a manifesto to Europe ; and it will tell.'

'I wonder what the fellow who made the invention will think of it all,' said the first. 'He will see that he is not to have it all his own way, but that the country will have its say in the matter.'

'What can the country do? You can buy a machine if you like, or you can let it alone. That's all the country has to say to it.'

'Why, if this thing becomes common, it will ruin all the railways, and you will see they won't allow that without a fight.'

'But what can they do, any more than the old coaching proprietors could keep out steam?'

'The old coaching proprietors hadn't a powerful division of M.P.'s at their back, as the railways have, to say nothing of the shipowners, who would suffer too. And look at the millions of money invested in railways everywhere, which would be made worthless at a blow. There's a great panic on the Stock Exchange already, and it's nothing to what's coming. No Government could afford to let such a thing go on without control. They would be out of office in a week.'

'Their successors couldn't hinder it either,' said the other. 'It's no use fighting against invention and progress. You Tories always think you are going to dam Niagara with a pitchfork.'

'You Liberals would go for anything new, no matter if it ruined the country. Where would England be if railway shares went down fifty per cent.? It would make a nation of paupers.'

'She would be ten times richer than before. If the new invention is to displace the old, you may be sure it is because it is worth more, and will pay better. If it do not, it is not going to supersede railways. If it do, the country will be all the richer.'

'That may be in the long run,' said another ; 'but in the meantime the millions invested in railways would be lost to their owners, and you may be sure they will not submit to that if they can help it.'

'Besides,' said the speaker of Conservative sympathies, 'look at the effect it would have on foreign relations. What could hinder the French or Germans from landing an army where they please? It would be twice as bad as the Channel Tunnel, and there's no mistaking what the opinion of the country was about that. It won't do; the Government must interfere. It would simply be the ruin of the country if other nations got hold of it.'

'Well, then, the country must be ruined, for it's simply impossible to prevent their getting hold of it sooner or later. How on earth could it be prevented, if the thing is to be used at all?'

'By the Government buying the invention, and keeping it a dead secret in their own hands.'

'A pretty penny they would have to pay for it! If the secret were mine, I wouldn't sell it for a farthing less than a million. Who's to find the money? The British taxpayer, of course.'

'And precious cheap at the price! You

Radicals are always thinking of money and
expense, and how you can save a halfpenny
here and three farthings there. You wouldn't
spend sixpence to sew up a hole in your pocket
that sovereigns were slipping out of.'

'Suppose he wouldn't sell, or asks too much?
Where would you be then?'

'Catch him refusing! He'll be precious glad
to get the Government for a customer. You
won't find many fellows to refuse a cool
million.'

'You will though, when he might make two
millions, or ten, by getting the public for a customer : and this fellow will be a fool if he does
anything else.'

'Well, if he won't sell to the nation, he can't
be allowed to sell to the public, that's all. Sir
Edward Watkin wasn't allowed to make his
Channel Tunnel, and this is just a parallel
case. Private interest must yield to public
necessity.'

'Yes ; but then the Government knew where
to catch Sir Edward Watkin. How are they

going to catch this fellow? Throw salt on his
tail, I suppose?'

'Enough of golden salt will catch him, I
warrant; but if that doesn't do, they must
manage to cage him somehow.'

I went up to my room, it may well be supposed, with my head whirling. I seemed to be
immeshed in a network of interests, of political
hopes and fears and dangers which became
more entangled and inexplicable the more I
thought of it. My head swam at the estimate
of the pecuniary value of my secret given by
men who were evidently familiar with financial
matters; my wildest dreams of profit had never
reached such a height as their careless conversation disclosed. But I had thought very little
of profit; my dreams had been of knowledge,
of the advance of science, of extended intercourse among men, of human brotherhood, of
universal peace. How contemptible seemed all
the speculations to which I had listened—all
the issues I had heard raised that day! My
father's dreams of freedom and national in-

dependence were noble and disinterested in comparison, mad and hopeless as I deemed them. But how to steer a prudent course? how to make my way safely through the complications that surrounded me? One thing only could I determine on—that I would not make my secret the property of any Government, for any bribe that could be offered me.

On coming down the next morning, I found the breakfast-room deserted, all the other lodgers having gone off to business. The table was covered with the morning newspapers, and while waiting for my rasher and cup of coffee, I had time to glance over their contents. In all of them I found my exploit of the previous day announced in leaded type, with the usual sensational headings, and each devoted a leader to the subject.

The *Times* enlarged upon the benefits that must ultimately accrue from so brilliant a discovery, and admitted that it must in time come into general use, not only in England, but over the world. 'But the Government is bound to see,' it concluded, 'that the change is effected in such a manner as neither to injure existing commercial interests nor to imperil the safety of the country. Already the symptoms of a serious panic are visible, and if it be permitted to attain the dimensions to which it threatens to grow unless instant action be taken to reassure investors, the most serious financial embarrassment is certain to result. This is a matter of immediate and pressing importance. Still more urgent is the necessity of providing that the security of our insular position be not affected. This will doubtless engage the attention of military experts, to whom it must be left to devise a plan by which all the undoubted advantages of the new method of locomotion may be reaped, without surrendering the still greater advantage of our unique position in Europe. We are glad to observe, from the statesmanlike speech of the Chancellor of the Exchequer last night, that the Government are fully alive to their responsibilities at this juncture.'

The *Standard* applauded the resolution of the Government, as conveyed in the words of their spokesman, the Chancellor of the Exchequer, to deal firmly and promptly with the crisis that had so suddenly arisen. 'The interests of England must be their only guide ; and these, whatever may be said by unpractical doctrinaires and cosmopolites who overflow with regard for every country but their own, are by no means identical with the equalisation of scientific powers and advantages over all the world.'

The *Daily Telegraph* hailed the invention as the greatest, the most striking, the most far-reaching in its consequences that had been made for centuries. 'Even the steam-engine and the telegraph must yield to it in interest and importance. To find its parallel we must go back to the time when, as ancient myths relate, Prometheus stole the sacred flame from heaven ; or, as our modern sages prefer to put it, the hairy ancestor of man discovered that he could make fire by the friction of two sticks ;

to the first canoe that was launched, or the first house that was built. This is one of the primeval, gigantic, elemental discoveries that go down to the roots of man's condition in this world, and looks as startling, among the puny contrivances of which we are so vain, as a mammoth or a mastodon would do among latter-day cows and horses. It is the opening of a new era.'

The *Daily News* considered that a great step had been made in civilisation, which would be memorable not only for what was yet to come, but also for what must be left behind. A great revolution was inaugurated, whose effects would be felt not only in the commercial and industrial worlds, but in society, in politics, in international relations, and in every department of practical life. ' To talk of controlling such a change in the interest of any class or any nation, as the Chancellor of the Exchequer did last night, is as idle as it was for Canute to pretend to control the rising of the tide. Great interests may, and no doubt will, be affected. Old relations be-

tween nations, old methods of attack and defence may, and no doubt will, become obsolete.
But such changes must be met by courage, by
foresight, by a frank adoption and adaptation
of new powers to meet new dangers, and not by
cowardly outcry, or by any vain attempt to
sweep back the rising tide with the mop of
official interference. If the latter impossible
feat is to be attempted, as it would seem it is,
we shall soon see the Conservative Mrs Parting-
tons swept away amid the derision and contempt of the civilised world.'

I laid down the papers, and tried to think
calmly of my position, and to sketch a plan of
action to guide me in the interview to which I
momentarily expected a summons. It was clear
that the Cabinet would be compelled by their
own supporters to try to establish some control
over my action, and that they would insist on
my doing nothing until they should have settled
how much liberty it would suit them to accord
to me. If I refused, what then? How far were
they prepared to go in the direction of coercion?

Was it wise to trust myself in their hands so far as to go to a place of their own appointment, where I might be practically imprisoned for the time? On the other hand, by openly distrusting them, I should be declaring war, and incurring not only their hostility but that of their supporters, who were a majority of the public to whom I had to look. I had decided at last to go, although I felt all the old hatred with which in my Irish home I had learnt to regard them, rising strong within my breast.

CHAPTER X.

DEFIANCE.

T was now ten o'clock, and no message had arrived. Wearying of inaction, I resolved to make a short excursion. Taking up the light bundle into which my wings were folded, I went out quietly, and walking on the Embankment, looked around for a quiet spot where I might fasten them on unnoticed. I was annoyed, however, to observe that the man who had come to my assistance the evening before was hanging about, and keeping near me. 'He wants another half-crown,' I thought, 'but he would have a better chance if he would frankly ask for it, instead of dogging my steps like this.' Finding I could not shake him off, I made up my mind to disregard him, and slipping behind a buttress of Waterloo Bridge, I proceeded to unstrap the wings and put them on. I was just securing the last buckle when he came up.

'Now, my good fellow,' said I, 'you must not hang about after me like this. If you want more money, say so, and I will give it you, but you must go about your business, and leave me to mine.'

'I beg your pardon, sir; I don't want any money. I was only just looking after you, like.'

'But I don't want you,' said I. 'I am safe enough now, in broad daylight, and I can take very good care of myself. I must trouble you to take yourself off, and leave me alone.'

'I don't know whether you can take care of yourself,' said he. 'I never see a gentleman go about with things like these,' laying hold of one of the wings rather rudely.

'Hands off!' cried I, angrily; 'I will give you in charge to the next policeman, if you don't let go at once.'

'Oh, you will, will you ?' said he, still retaining his hold, while with the other hand he produced a policeman's whistle, and blew a shrill note.

Immediately the truth flashed upon me, and the surprising ease with which he had routed my assailants of the previous evening was explained. It was clear the Home Secretary had put a detective to watch me the moment I left his room. In a sudden blaze of indignation I clenched my fist, and struck him with all my force right upon the nose. The blow was a severe one, and he staggered back. At the same time I heard footsteps rapidly running up, and springing up a few steps of the stone stair leading to the bridge, I launched myself into the air, just over the head of the approaching policeman, who grasped ineffectively at my feet as I rose.

Once afloat in what I was beginning to regard as my own element, I circled around at my ease, watching, not without amusement, the scene I had left below. I saw the policeman

I

pick up the fallen detective, who first applied a handkerchief to his nose, and then shook his fist at me with a volley of oaths. I saw a crowd gather with surprising quickness, and, angry as I was with the attempted restriction upon my liberty, I resolved to give a sufficiently public exhibition of my powers.

I accordingly called all my resources into play. I flew low along the surface of the river, almost dipping my feet in the water as I passed beneath one of the arches of the bridge. I winged my way slowly up the stream as far as Westminster, and then turning, swept with my utmost speed as far down as London Bridge. Then returning to where the crowd was densest, I rose with wide spiral sweeps upwards, the roar of voices growing fainter and fainter until it was lost in the distance, while the river seemed a mere silver thread lying a mile below, and I must myself have been almost, if not quite, lost to the view of the gazing multitude. I felt a proud and exhilarating sense of freedom as I surveyed the city spread like a huge anthill beneath me, and tried to make out the exact position of Whitehall and Downing Street. 'That is where a dozen crawling wingless insects are sitting at this moment,' I soliloquised, 'to determine whether they will allow me to give these powers to men, or even to exercise them myself. Why should I hold myself at their beck and call? They have forfeited all claim to courtesy at my hands; let them come to me if they want to see what I can do. I will trust them no further; I laugh at their puny authority. What is to hinder me from crossing yonder " silver streak " that shines on the far horizon? ay, or even the Atlantic itself, to the home of freedom beyond? Freedom! ah, can I forget the land that lies dark under their shadow, only a few strokes to the west? Let them look to it, or I may remember I am an Irishman still.'

Not wishing to descend openly as I had risen, I made a wide circuit towards the north, searching for a quiet spot. The solitude of Epping Forest attracted me, and descending in a

lonely part of it, I divested myself of my
wings, and folded them up into a parcel. I
then found my way to Chingford Station, from
which I took my ticket to the city.

My first care was to secure a quiet lodging.
Avoiding the Strand district, I found a couple
of suitable rooms in one of the sleepy Blooms-
bury streets to the west of the British Museum.
I then went out and purchased a locked tin
box, large enough to contain my precious
parcel. This secured, I strolled out, lunched
at one of the Holborn chop-houses, and made
my way from thence to the *Echo* office.

I found the editor busy at his desk.   He
jumped up and shook me warmly by the hand.

'I knew it!' said he; 'I knew you weren't
going to sneak off. We were just getting in all
the accounts we could of your doings this morning. The evening papers will be full of them.
We have a grand report of your flight from the
Embankment, and your disappearance in the
clouds ; we have had the detective interviewed,
and our reporter is trying to draw the Home

Secretary at this moment. Everyone will have it you are off for good, and that the next thing we shall hear is, that you have made terms with the French or German Government. I was sure you wouldn't do that, for you can get far better terms here if you hold out for them. What is your next move? Open defiance, I suppose, or you would never have come here.'

' I mean to let the public know exactly how I have been treated,' said I ; 'I hope you can give me space for that. I will then say that on no terms whatever will I put my invention at the disposal of this or any other Government, but that it shall be free and open to all the world ; and I will appeal to the people of all countries to support and protect me.'

' Bravo ! that's the right and truly liberal line to take, and must win in the long run. But you'll have a hard fight of it. "Jingoism" is greatly in the ascendant just now, especially in London, and three-fourths of the press will be down on you as a traitor and a public enemy.'

'Well, give me the slips and let me fall to at once,' said I, drawing a chair to the desk.

'We'll let the first edition go out as it is,' said he; 'it is sensational enough in all conscience. Then we will announce a special, and come out with your article, which will run like a prairie fire. I should like, though, to wait for the official disclaimer we are almost certain to get from the Home Secretary. It will be very damaging if we can put that in the same number.'

The reporter returned while I was writing, but without the intelligence that had been hoped for. The Home Secretary, he said, had refused to see him, the Cabinet having been suddenly summoned to meet under circumstances of the gravest anxiety; and he was given to understand that the request for special information on the part of the *Echo* was an impertinence.

'Better and better!' exclaimed the editor, and fell to work on an article denouncing the high-handed tyranny and general profligacy and corruption of the Tory Government.

CHAPTER XI.

REBELLION.

THE new edition did indeed 'run like a prairie fire.' In addition to articles upon the topic which in the morning had been all-absorbing, it contained news from Ireland of such gravity as to eclipse even that in interest. The first telegrams were of course fragmentary and meagre; but they made it clear that a serious outbreak had occurred; and subsequent reports not only confirmed the first outlines that had been given, but amplified and enlarged every detail. It was not for a day or two that a connected and authentic narrative of what had happened was in the hands of the public; but I must here anticipate my own adventures a little, in order to give a consecutive history of events which had no little influence on my career.

It appeared that at a place called Killynure, in County Donegal, only a few miles from the spot where I had been born and brought up, an extensive eviction was impending. It was on so large a scale that resistance was expected, and an unusually large force—fifty mounted policemen and the same number of foot-soldiers—accompanied the landlord and resident magistrates to the scene of action, in order to enforce the execution of the law. On arriving at the place, they found collected a large body of the surrounding peasantry, most of whom were armed with rifles and revolvers. Some preparations had evidently been made for defence, the walls of the cottages and outhouses had been loopholed, and groups of men, placed with a good deal of skill, occupied the hedges and ditches, and other points affording cover and protection. To the command to disperse they replied by a defiant refusal, and a threat to fire if a stick or stone were disturbed. To overawe them by a display of superior force, the soldiers and policemen were ordered to advance to the nearest cottage, around which they were drawn up. A ladder was placed against the roof, and a number of labourers, who accompanied the expedition in the capacity of a 'crowbar brigade,' were directed to begin operations by stripping off the thatch.

Before any of them could mount to obey the order, a voice from among the crowd called out,—

'The first man who sets foot on that ladder will be shot dead! I give you fair warning. Remember Tom Crawford—beware!'

The man with the crowbar hung back.

'Bedad, sir,' he said to the magistrate in command, 'this is more than I bargained for.'

'Do your duty at once,' was the reply.

'Begorra, the divil a bit I'll be shot for your divarsion!' said the man. 'Them fellows never misses their aim. Go up yourself and see how you'll like it.'

'Put the coward in irons!' roared the R.M., 'and send the next man up.'

But the next man had no more stomach for the job than his mate, and the whole squad of labourers flatly refused to move hand or foot. In vain the leaders stormed and threatened.

'Send some of the soldiers; they're paid to take their lives in their hands,' was the only reply.

The young lieutenant commanding the soldiers was hot-headed and impetuous.

'Get out of the way, ye Irish cowards!' he exclaimed, indignantly. 'Are ye frightened by a pack of bog-trotters? Give me the crowbar!' and in another moment he was seen on the ridge of the roof, with his crowbar raised to plant in the thatch.

'His blood is on his own head!' cried the voice that had spoken before.

The sharp crack of a rifle rang out upon the morning air, and the young officer, dropping the crowbar, rolled down the slope of the roof and fell heavily to the ground.

A yell of rage arose from the soldiers, and five or six of them, without waiting for orders, fired wildly in the direction whence the shot had come. One or two men were seen to fall, but in a moment the shots were returned with telling effect from a different quarter, and several redcoats rolled on the ground. Their comrades, with shouts of execration, began loading and firing as fast as they could handle their cartridges ; the peasantry replied coolly and steadily, and at a murderous advantage, for they were sheltered by the banks and hedges, and from every cottage wall the flashes blazed through window and loophole. The fight became general, and on every side was heard the cracking of unexpected rifles, as every rock, every bush of gorse, and every clump of thorns sent forth its ambushed occupants. It was clear that every point of vantage had been occupied, and the sides of the little valley lined by a numerous body of well-armed and determined men. The police, conspicuous on horseback, were at a still greater disadvantage than the soldiers, and were

unable to charge with effect among the trees
and tall hedges that shut in the place on every
side.   Within two minutes every officer had
fallen, and the men began to realise that they
were in a trap.   Nearly a third of their number
lay on the ground, and the rest had lost their
ranks, and stood huddled together into a mere
mob, exposed on every side to the fire of their
assailants.

'Will you lay down your arms?' cried the
man who seemed to act as leader to the peasantry.   'Lay down your arms, and you shall
have free quarter.   If you do not, we won't
leave a man of you alive!'

There was no officer to give the word, but the
firing stopped.   Then from every hedge and
wall around were seen the levelled tubes of
loaded rifles converging upon the entrap-
ped and beaten crowd.   The leader spoke
again,—

'Every man throw down his rifle and hold his
hands over his head.   I give you ten seconds,
and I'll not bid you twice.   At the word ten we

fire. One — two — three — four — five — six — seven—'

The last words were drowned in the rattle of the dropping rifles, as the stern order was obeyed.

'Now form in fours, and march down the lane and through the gate into the middle of the meadow. Attention! Quick march!' and with an approach to military precision the soldiers sullenly obeyed, leaving the ground strewed with their weapons and the dead bodies of their comrades.

'Halt!' and they found themselves drawn up unarmed in the centre of a small field, surrounded on every side by armed and victorious enemies. A dozen men were told off to collect the rifles and bayonets, and another dozen to relieve the prisoners of their cartridge belts and pouches. The police were compelled to dismount, and their horses led off. The leader spoke again,—

'We have you under fire. We cannot keep you as prisoners. We do not want your blood.

You may go, one by one. Each man, as he passes the gate, must swear an oath not to bear arms against Ireland. Those who swear will be allowed to pass ; those who refuse will be shot. Right file, front rank, march to the gate and swear.'

The first soldier marched to the gate, where the oath was tendered by a man with a bible in one hand and a cocked revolver in the other. He swore, and passed out. The second did the same. So did everyone. There were no officers to set an example of refusal, and the rifles were levelled with a pitiless accuracy of aim they had learned to dread. They made no attempt to re-form their ranks, but straggled down the road in a broken and disorganised crowd, from which it was believed there were many desertions before they reached the town from which they had marched in the morning. They left behind all their officers, and between thirty and forty private soldiers and policemen, dead, as well as the two resident magistrates and the evicting landlord.

Such was the narrative of the newspaper correspondents, gathered from the story told by the men themselves, and the rumours that spread like wildfire through the country. All accounts agreed in stating that the insurgents had showed remarkable steadiness and discipline, and were evidently under bold and skilful leadership. And all took note of the significant circumstance, that every officer on the ground, commissioned and non-commissioned, had been shot down at the very beginning of the affray.

CHAPTER XII.

THREATENINGS AND SLAUGHTER.

THE excitement produced by this intelligence was overpowering. Even the events of the previous day and of that morning were well-nigh forgotten. I had determined not to venture again into the neighbourhood of the House of Commons; but drawn by an irresistible attraction, I found myself at about four P.M. one of a vast concourse of people who filled Palace Yard, besieged all the approaches to the House, and fought for entrance into Westminster Hall and the outer lobbies. With the utmost difficulty the police were able to open a way through the densely-packed crowd for the admission of members when they arrived. Every now and then a roar of cheers announced the arrival of some popular hero, or a chorus of groans and hisses greeted such as were suspected of Irish sympathies. There was no doubt of the direction in which popular feeling flowed, and it was shown in a practical manner on the arrival of the first Irish member who was recognised. No sooner was his name called out by someone in the crowd than there was a sudden rush, he was dragged out of his hansom, and received a dozen blows from as many patriotic fists and walking-sticks. With a good deal of difficulty he was rescued by the police, and carried into Westminster Hall with blood dropping down his face, and his coat hanging in shreds about him.

In the confusion I had forced my way into the hall, where for two or three hours I remained wedged in a dense crowd, unable either to get out or to make my way further in. Meanwhile the rumours flew thick and fast among them. At first the Irish leader had been lynched by a mob who had besieged his house from the first

K

moment the news was known. 'And serve him right!' was the general verdict; 'he's at the bottom of it all!' By-and-by the report was that he had not come out at the expected time, that his house had been broken into, when it was found he had escaped by the back. Presently the word spread that all the Irish members then present in the House had been arrested by a special order, and were being conveyed to prison. By this time I found myself tightly jammed against the door of the members' entrance, leading from the side of the hall, and the pressure of the crowd was so great that I could hardly breathe. I felt the door yielding behind me, and, as the strain increased with a sudden movement of the mass, it burst open, and I fell through into the passage beyond. A perfect avalanche of human bodies fell over me, and, under the intolerable pressure, I fainted from pain and suffocation. I marvel to this day that I was not killed on the spot.

I was not killed, however. The sharp pain

that roused me to consciousness was caused by the surgeon's fingers as he felt my fractured ribs. Three of them had yielded, and my face and body were discoloured with bruises.

'He will do now,' said the doctor. 'There is no injury to the lung. But he must be kept very quiet, and not allowed to move.'

Was I in a hospital? I thought not. And yet it was plain it was not a private house. The little iron bedstead on which I lay accorded ill with the other furniture of the room, which was of varnished pine, cushioned with stuffed leather, and of modern-mediæval pattern. The window was perpendicular Gothic, with diamond panes, and evidently looked out on some vast empty space, for nothing was visible through it but the sky. The woman who moved about with business-like air was evidently a professional nurse, and wore the uniform of a hospital—I could not tell which.

'Am I badly hurt, doctor? How long may I expect to be laid up?'

'You have three ribs fractured; fortunately

the ends were not driven in on the lung, and they ought to be well enough to admit of your sitting up in about a fortnight. The rate of healing, of course, depends on many circumstances;' and he proceeded to ask me certain questions with reference to my habits of life, family, etc. 'That is very satisfactory,' said he, 'and we may hope to have you up in the shortest possible time.'

'Am I in a hospital?' I inquired.

'No; you are in the Clock Tower of St Stephen's, the guest for the present. of the Home Secretary. He was present when the bodies were taken out of the passage, and fortunately recognised you, and ordered special attention to be paid to your case.'

'The bodies!'

'Ah, yes; it was a bad accident. There were four or five people trampled to death, and nearly a dozen more injured. You were at the very bottom, and it was well for you; it saved you from the feet of the crowd.'

For the next few days the doctor's injunction

was literally obeyed. I was kept very quiet indeed, being permitted to see no one except the nurse and my medical attendant. I was rapidly gaining strength, however, and at length my earnest request for newspapers was listened to. I found that my own case received a good deal of attention, and that daily bulletins were issued of my progress towards convalescence. It appeared to be understood that I was in a sort of honourable captivity ; indeed, the House had, by a unanimous vote, authorised the Home Secretary to keep me under restraint until the commission now sitting to determine the military value of my invention should have finished their labours.

That commission was engaged in taking the evidence of military and naval experts, and I turned with a good deal of curiosity to the reports of their proceedings. It seemed to be agreed on every hand that the possession of the invention by any foreign nation would expose England to so much risk of invasion as entirely to annihilate the advantages hitherto arising from her insular position and naval supremacy. She must be prepared, according to these authorities, to live in constant danger of invasion by forces vastly superior, in point of numbers, to any that she could put in the field —or rather in the air—against them. Even the safeguards which might be adopted in the case of a Channel Tunnel could be of no avail against an enemy who could select any point of attack he chose. Thus reasoned the military experts, and their opinion appeared to be producing a strong effect upon the public.

Most of the newspapers talked mere 'jingoism,' maintaining that England could not afford to sacrifice the advantages she enjoyed from her position, even for the sake of an invention so fascinating, and in other respects so useful. Many Liberal papers admitted that, although the danger was, in their opinion, grossly exaggerated, and all the counterbalancing advantages entirely ignored, nevertheless, so great was the folly of mankind, that the injury from constantly-recurring panics would more than neutralise the benefits to be reaped from a free use of the invention. The few papers, and still fewer public men, who argued that England could hold her own under any circumstances, and that even solicitude for her greatness and security would not excuse the crime against the human race involved in suppressing such a discovery, were denounced as traitorous and unpatriotic. The certainty of financial panic, and the danger of a serious and even ruinous monetary crisis, were also urged as a reason for not permitting the use of such a revolutionary invention, or of allowing it only under such restrictions as would prevent its coming into general use. The question, I could not fail to observe, was discussed without the slightest reference to my own feelings and opinions on the matter, or any hint that I had the smallest right to dispose of my own invention in my own way.

But even my own grievances were forgotten in the excitement of the news from Ireland.

Events had moved quickly during the week that followed my accident. First came the fullest confirmation of the news that had caused so much popular excitement. This was quickly followed by an affair of much greater magnitude, which altered the aspect of the whole matter, and made it impossible any longer to regard it as a mere local rising. It was evidently a carefully-organised and widespread insurrection, and the failure to recognise its true character had led to a disaster of a kind not easily retrieved. It had enabled the insurgents to score a decided success at the very outset, of which the moral effect was incalculable.

On the day after the 'Battle of Killynure,' as the first affair had been called, the entire military and police force at the disposal of the county authorities, to the number of about five hundred, had been collected, and on the second day they marched to complete the work that had been interrupted, and to chastise the insurgents, who still preserved an attitude of defiance. The latter, meanwhile, had not been idle. Defences had been extemporised, and when the attacking force arrived on the scene of the previous fight, they found themselves in front of a series of earthworks running right across the narrow valley in which the little hamlet was situated, while the heights on both sides were studded with rifle-pits and lined with sharpshooters. With almost incredible carelessness, considering the experience they had already had of the generalship of the insurgent leader, they made no examination of the ground in front of them, but marched right up the valley, until stopped by the rude ditches that had been thrown up to bar their way. Here they halted, and became unpleasantly aware that the trenches before them were filled with men and bristling with rifles.

The situation was realised too late. A second time they had walked into a trap with their eyes open. The leaders looked at each other blankly. Two resident magistrates, an

inspector and sub-inspector of police, a raw
and inexperienced captain, and two still rawer
lieutenants, with no very clearly understood
order of subordination among them, they were
well accustomed to the work of dispersing
mobs and of unroofing cabins, but the smell
of powder was not yet familiar to them. But
there was no retreat; and it would not do to
confess themselves out-generalled by a mere
peasant. They were foolish—rash; but they
were no cowards.

'In the Queen's name!' cried the senior
magistrate, riding forward, 'I command you to
lay down your arms and disperse. Anyone
taken with arms in his hands will be tried by
drum-head court-martial and shot. All surrendering their arms will be allowed to go
peaceably home.'

'You will have to lay down your own arms,'
responded the insurgent leader, partly rising
from behind an earthwork. 'Don't you see you
are in a trap? We don't make war with pop-
guns, and if your rifles are not piled within two

minutes we will open fire on you. Boys, cover
the officers.'

'Fix bayonets!' shouted the captain, 'and
carry the works at the double quick!'

'Fire!' was the answer, and a volley crashed
sharply out, echoing and re-echoing down the
steep and narrow valley.

For the second time every officer fell at the
first discharge. The men charged the steep
bank gallantly, but were met by such a close
and continuous fire from the Winchester rifles
with which the insurgents were armed, not only
from the front, but on both sides, that they were
forced to recoil. Again and again, with the
utmost bravery, men sprang out of the ranks
and tried to rally and lead them again to the
charge; but in every case these impromptu
leaders were coolly picked out and carefully
shot down by the marksmen on the slopes.
The fire of the assailants, directed against
enemies almost entirely hidden, was wild and
ineffective, while that of the defenders, coolly
taking aim from behind their entrenchments,

was terribly accurate and murderous. Such an affair could only last a few minutes. Hemmed in on three sides, opposed to an almost unseen enemy, and without leaders, the remainder of the force threw down their arms and surrendered. Almost half their number had fallen. To the rest the same oath was tendered as formerly, and taken. Their arms and ammunition fell into the hands of the victors.

The outburst of wrath evoked by the receipt of this news in England was tremendous. Everything else was forgotten in the stern demand for instant and exemplary punishment. A small but costly and perfectly-equipped expedition was at once organised and placed under the orders of the most famous and popular general in the country, who had often declared that nothing would better please him than the opportunity of crushing an Irish rebellion. He took down a map of the country, placed his finger on a certain spot, and said, 'Here they will try to make a stand. My telegram announcing their dispersal will be dated on the

——th of ——.' A royal duke consented to take command of one of the divisions, and popular confidence and enthusiasm at once revived. The few croakers who hinted that it is not always safe to despise an enemy; that the Irish seemed this time to have got what they never had before—a general; that our own commander, famous and successful as his career had been, had never yet been matched against a man of real military genius; and that even royalty was not an absolute guarantee for good fortune and success, were shouted down. No counsels of moderation or compromise could be so much as listened to until the honour of England had been vindicated, and her authority established beyond dispute.

How shall I go on to relate the history of the next few weeks? I know little of campaigning, and in my solitary room I had no means of gaining information but the newspapers, which indeed I saw every day, but knew not how far to believe. I saw nothing, either of the fierce excitement which seethed and boiled

in the streets from day to day, although the
roar of the multitudes that congregated in and
around Palace Yard often came to my ears.
So far as I was able at the time to follow the
course of events, it was something like this :—

The entire country, with the solitary exception of the town of Belfast, declared for the
insurgents immediately upon the result of the
second encounter in Donegal becoming known.
Every railway line and telegraph wire was
seized, and the English garrisons in the different towns where they were stationed, were
at once in a state of siege, and masters only of
the ground they stood on. As yet none of
them had surrendered ; but with most of the
railways destroyed, and the country swarming
with an armed and hostile population, their
position was every day becoming more pre-
carious. On the very day after the victory in
Donegal, the rebel leader put three hundred
picked and well-armed men in a train, swept
up to Belfast in two hours, and was master of
all the railway stations in the town before the

inhabitants had fully made up their minds whether to believe the news of the previous day or not. A Provisional Government was set up in Dublin, having as president the ex-chief of the Irish parliamentary party, who had escaped from London on the night of my accident, and crossed the channel in an open boat the day after ; several of his followers, who had attempted to cross by the usual routes, had been arrested and lodged in prison. In short, the whole country was in the hands of the insurgents, and for a time there was a lull in the storm, while the expedition which was to crush the rebellion was being prepared. The English, on their part, so soon as the first wild burst of rage was over, awaited with confidence the result of the expedition, which they determined should deliver a crushing blow, and put an end at once, and for ever to even the possibility of an Irish rising.

CHAPTER XIII.

IMPRISONED.

IT was during this lull that I had my first interview with the Home Secretary in his character of host, or rather gaoler. I was now able to sit up, and was in my favourite place beside the window, the lower part of which was open, and overlooked the terrace and the river from the third storey, when he was announced.

I arose and bowed stiffly, without a word.

'Come,' said he genially, 'you must not be offended at what, if you knew the world better, you would be aware was the most ordinary measure of precaution, and quite unavoidable on the part of the Government. I am heartily sorry you should have had any reason to complain of rudeness on the part of the officer we placed on duty.'

'It is the officer himself I complain of, and not his conduct,' said I. 'But let that pass. I wish now to thank you for your hospitality, and to say that, as I am quite able to move about, I do not wish to trespass on it any further.'

'My dear sir,' he answered, 'it is no trespass whatever. We are happy to have been able to serve you so far, and are desirous of serving you still further. I have come, in fact, to arrange with you for your setting to work, as soon as you have sufficiently recovered, in the manufacture of machines similar to the one you have so successfully exhibited. The Government will place every facility at your disposal, including workmen and materials, and will, in fact, make you chief of a department in one of the royal arsenals, at a handsome salary. They are prepared, in addition, to offer you a large reward for the invention, which they recognise

L

as one of the most remarkable of modern times.'

'Mr Secretary,' I replied, ' I have already said, as publicly as I can, that I will not enter into any agreement, either with this or any other Government, to place my invention at their disposal. It is to the general public I shall look for support.'

' We think,' said he, ' that you have not sufficiently considered the danger to the State involved in the too sudden diffusion of such a power as your invention would put into the hands of other and possibly hostile countries, if rashly brought into general use. And we hope that, when the very liberal terms we are prepared to concede are made known to you, you will no longer hesitate to enter upon a course dictated alike by patriotic feeling and a natural regard for your own interest.'

'I don't care what the terms may be,' I replied ; ' my resolution is the same.'

' I am authorised by Her Majesty's Government to offer you one hundred thousand

pounds for your invention, and a salary of
two thousand pounds a year as long as you
continue to manufacture machines under their
sole direction. They will, of course, expect
you to enter into an engagement to supply
no one but themselves, either the general
public or any foreign Government.'

'I would not accept the terms if they offered
me a million,' I replied, 'so we may dismiss
the subject.'

'Have you considered the consequences of
refusal?' said he. 'You cannot suppose that
the Government, in view of the public danger
which, in their judgment, would result from
a general use of your machines, are prepared
to abandon that control which they exercise
for the good of the State, over the actions of
every one of its members? They cannot, con-
sistently with their public duty, allow you
to scatter your machines broadcast over the
country, to be taken up, as they would immediately be, by every other Government
in Europe. If you will not work in their

service, they cannot allow you to work at all.'

'And pray, Mr Secretary, how do they propose to prevent it ? They may forbid my manufacturing or selling machines in England. But England is not the only place in the world.'

'Exactly,' said he; 'it is not. And for that very reason they will feel it to be their duty to prevent you from making and selling them anywhere. In plain words, they cannot set you at liberty without an understanding that you will accede to their terms. Any price in reason, or even out of reason, will be paid for your invention ; but out of their hands it shall not be permitted to go.'

'So, Mr Secretary, this high-minded and patriotic Government are prepared to imprison for life a man who has committed no crime, but, on the contrary, has made a remarkable˙ discovery, and conferred a benefit on the race ! The thing is absurd ; no Government dare do anything of the kind ; no people would stand it for an hour! Go and tell the House of Commons and the country what you are going to do, and see what they will say to it. Stay— I'll do it myself!' I exclaimed, sitting down to the table, and drawing a pen and ink towards me.

'What are you doing?' demanded the Home Secretary.

'I am going to write a letter to the *Times*, in which I will give an exact report of the conversation we have just had, and let the public form their own opinion of it.'

'Then I must tell you,' said he, 'that no such communication will be allowed to pass beyond these walls.'

'I knew you dared not act in open day,' said I. 'If the reasons for the course you are taking are so convincing to the Government, why should they not convince the people too? I will tell you : because they are always jealous for individual liberty. And they will be so in the present case. I refuse your offer, and I despise your threats. You dare not carry them out ; and I can wait until the truth is known.'

'I will leave you now,' said the Secretary ; 'and I hope that a little reflection will convince you that the proposals of the Government are reasonable, and indeed necessary. You are likely to have sufficient leisure to reconsider your determination ; and, in spite of what you have said, I have no doubt that, on second thoughts, you will accept our terms. If you do, you shall find us munificent patrons.'

There was a meaning emphasis on the last sentence ; but I merely stood up and bowed coldly as he left the room.

In spite of the bold front I had tried to maintain, I was by no means confident that the immediate verdict of popular feeling would be in my favour. The British public was in one of its periodic fits of Jingoism, intensified to fever heat by the situation in Ireland ; and I knew that there was a very general desire that the new invention should be employed and tested in the approaching campaign. Our

great military authority, in his evidence before
the Royal Commission, had expressed the
opinion that it would be simply invaluable in
the field ; and it was an open secret that he
had already prepared elaborate plans for its
employment in transport and outpost duty, as
well as in actual battle. I was more and more
determined every day, however, that he should
not have the chance of putting them into
execution. The more I thought of the action
of the Government, the more indignant I became. I found myself following every detail
of the insurgent movement in Ireland with the
keenest interest and sympathy.

'Why did I not cast in my lot with them
when I had the chance?' I bitterly asked myself a hundred times a day. 'Why did I ever
come to this selfish and ungrateful country? I
am justly punished for my own want of
patriotism.'

I loathed the abundant, even sumptuous fare
with which I was provided every day, and
longed to share the coarse and scanty rations

of those brave campaigners. I would have re-joiced to exchange my comfortable room for the tenth part of a ragged tent, my luxurious bed for half a tattered blanket, shared with my compatriots.

My chief resource and consolation during this dreary time were in the newspapers, in which was certainly no lack of interest and excite-ment, and of encouragement as well. The expedition started in due time, but without the new and irresistible weapon which its leader had hoped to be the first to use. Its first task was the relief of the beleaguered garrison of Belfast, which still held out, and the establishment of a base of operations among the 'loyal' population still supposed to exist in considerable numbers in the northern province. And this was accom-plished with what appeared to be such ridiculous ease and quickness, that the rebellion seemed to have collapsed in a day, and men began to look at each other and wonder why they had allowed another trumpery little Irish rising so to disturb their equanimity. It was only necessary partially to bombard Belfast from a distance of six or seven miles, after which a landing was effected without resistance, and the town was found to have been evacuated by the insurgents.

When, however, an attempt was made to advance into the country, the difficulties of the campaign commenced. Everywhere the railways had been completely destroyed; not merely torn up for a few hundred yards, but rendered impassable for miles; even the ordinary roads had been treated in the same way. And at every point of obstruction swarms of sharpshooters descended almost at a moment's notice, as numerous, as annoying, and as difficult to strike as clouds of wasps. In vain it was attempted to clear the country in advance by flying bodies of cavalry, by shells, by rockets, by machine guns. The dragoons were invariably shot down almost to a man; the artillerymen shared the same fate, the guns being several times silenced from sheer lack of men to work them. After two or three weeks' fruitless endeavour to bring the rebels to an

engagement, the system of tactics pursued by
their leader began to be apparent, and, in spite
of the almost daily 'defeats' in which large
bodies of insurgents had retired before the
regular troops, it was clear that he had a
very definite plan, and that it was proving to
be a successful one. He depended entirely
upon the accuracy of his men's shooting at
long ranges, and upon their individual cool-
ness and resource rather than their steadiness
in large and disciplined masses.. And the accuracy of the Irish—or, as some began to
insist, the American—shooting, was wonderful.
Hardly a shot ever seemed to be thrown away.
Worst and most galling of all, the very first to
fall, even in the merest skirmish, were always
the officers.   It was quite clear that they were
designedly picked out ; and so uniformly fatal
to them was almost any kind of movement
in the face even of the most insignificant body
of the enemy, that ugly stories began to be
whispered of the demoralisation that was beginning to spread.   These were fiercely con-

tradicted; but, at the same time, special correspondents were placed under the severest restrictions by the general in command, who had never been an admirer of war correspondents, and liked them now less than ever.

In short, after three weeks' hard fighting with an almost impalpable enemy, the army had advanced about twelve miles in the direction of Portadown, which was the next point aimed at, and were masters of Belfast, and of the ground on which they stood. By a course of almost daily victories they had lost a fourth of their number, and three-fourths of their officers. A demand for reinforcements came at last, and some of the newspapers began sharply to question the ability of the general to whom the command had been entrusted, while Radical prints openly eulogised the Irish leader, and sneeringly asked why the royal duke who accompanied the expedition, and who was known to be burning with military ardour, and to possess unusual tactical ability, was not allowed to try his hand against the peasant general, or at least to lead his own division in the field.

During those three weeks my body ate, drank, and slept in London, but my spirit lived in Belfast and the surrounding country, where I had spent four years of student life, and where every hill, and grove, and by-road was familiar to me. How living and graphic the meagre telegrams and letters of the war correspondents became to me as I followed every movement, and pictured every commanding point along the roads and hillsides, from which I seemed to hear the ring of the rebel rifles, and to see their swift and stealthy movements! How I cursed my own forced inactivity, and the self-ishness and blindness and high-flown sentiment which had led me into my present position! I was in no mood to listen to the proposals with which I was now besieged by the Government. I was at last plainly offered a million by the Home Secretary, and, on my refusing it, I was given to understand that even that did not represent the ultimate limit of national generosity. But I stood firm, although I had no hope that the public, in their present mood, would condemn the course the Government was taking, and although I was now playfully challenged by the Secretary to appeal to them against my gaolers.

It appeared plain that I was doomed to a lengthened term of incarceration, and my heart sank as time went on, as I saw the measures that were now being systematically concerted for the reduction of Ireland by an overwhelming force and a strict blockade, and thought what effectual aid I could bring if I were only at liberty. It was too clear that the big battalions must win in the long run, and that all resistance, however heroic and skilfully conducted must in the end be beaten down.

CHAPTER XIV.

ESCAPE.

I HAD now abandoned all hope of being set at liberty either by the spontaneous action of the Government, or by the influence of public opinion upon them, and was vainly striving to reconcile myself to the inevitable, when the means of escape presented itself from an unexpected quarter. My Irish friends had not forgotten me, and while I was chafing at the restraints which prevented me from giving them any aid more effectual than passive sympathy, they were actively working with a view to my release. It was to the boldness and ingenuity of my brother Dick that I owed the opportunity of which I was fortunately able to avail myself.

It was almost midnight on a dark, hot, stifling evening in the latter end of August, and I sat at the open lattice of my window, watching the vivid flashes of lightning which at intervals lighted up the river beneath, and the buildings of St Thomas' Hospital on the other side. Too heated to care to go to bed, I was waiting for the cooling rain which presently began to fall in large drops, and which in a few minutes was coming down in such torrents as are rarely seen except in tropical climates.

A blinding flash dazzled my eyes for a moment, and I could almost have sworn I felt it lift the hair from my brow. Certainly something had glanced past me through the open window ; and, turning round, I was surprised to see an arrow lying on the floor. A piece of paper was fastened round it and a cord attached to the end, which passed out through the window. Unrolling the paper, I read the words ' Pull on this string.'

Hastily turning down my light, that I might not be seen at the window, I began to draw in the line. A few yards came freely. Then I felt I was lifting a weight, and presently a good-sized object came up to the lattice, which I easily lifted into the room.

To close my shutter and turn up the light was the work of a moment. My fingers were trembling with eagerness as I opened the parcel, for I already guessed what it contained. I could hardly restrain a shout of triumph as I grasped once more the pair of wings which I had first made, and left behind when I went from my father's house. Attached to the parcel was another scrap of paper, on which was scrawled in pencil, ' I am waiting in a boat below—Dick.'

The policeman who was responsible for my safe custody had already made his nightly visit, so I did not fear interruption. I fastened on the wings at my leisure ; then I turned out the light and opened my shutter. It was still raining, and dark, heavy clouds brooded low over the river ; but the thunder only rumbled at long intervals in the distance. My great fear was lest with my wings I should find myself unable to pass through the narrow lattice of the window. It was a close fit ; however, I was able to squeeze through, and, with an ecstacy of joy I cannot paint, I found myself at last outside my prison-wall, floating upon the free air.

I hovered a moment outside the window trying to fasten the lattice ; but the catch was inside, and I could not make it snap. I carried off the arrow and the string, but was obliged to leave the window open, a mute witness of the way by which I had taken my departure. Then turning into the friendly darkness, and guided by the sheen of the water, I took my way down stream, leaving the policeman on his weary beat up and down the wet and gliste ing terrace below.

As I flew low over the reach of open water lying between Westminster and Charing Cross bridges, I heard a low whistle, and wheeling

M

around once or twice, I made out, amid the confusing multitude of reflected lights, a small boat, rowed by one man, slowly dropping down the current. A moment's scrutiny was enough, and, carefully alighting in the stern, I grasped the hand which Dick extended.

'Don't say a word just now,' said he, in a low voice; 'I have had the greatest dodging to avoid the notice of the police on the Embankment. If it had not been such a wet and stormy night, I should never have been able to get near you. I have been trying it every night for a fortnight past, and never had a decent chance till now.'

'How did you know where to find me?' I asked, in the same tone.

'Oh, that was easy enough; everybody knew where you were confined, and it was, in fact, a favourite amusement to watch you sitting at your window at nights, where you might be very plainly seen after the gas was turned on. I have been down on the bridge myself night after night, and saw you frequently; but there were always so many people about that I could never venture to do anything to attract your attention, so I spent the time cudgelling my brains to think of some way of sending you a letter, and at last I thought of fastening one to an arrow and shooting it into your room. I bought a bow and arrows, and spent several mornings in archery practice, until I was able to shoot well enough to be sure I should not be in any danger of missing the window. But I had to wait for a wet night ; and, when one came, I was in mortal fear lest your window should not be open. I knew there would be a thunderstorm to-night, so I went in the evening and hired this boat at London Bridge, and I have been rowing back and forward for hours in it, waiting for a chance.'

'Have you laid any plans for our getting back to Ireland ? '

'No ; I could do nothing till I had got you out. But you can have no trouble. You can start whenever you like, and I will be able to make my way back somehow.'

'But, Dick, I have another pair of wings in town, which we can easily get. You might easily learn to use them, and we could go together.'

'I'm afraid not; you should have seen the vain attempts I made to use those you have, which seem to come as natural to you as if you were a bird. You may be sure we did our best to make use of them, but we had to give it up. I nearly broke my neck a dozen times.'

'I am quite sure I could teach you in a couple of lessons; it's the simplest thing in the world when you know the way.'

By this time we had dropped a good way down the river, and found no difficulty in running ashore and landing among the wharves above London Bridge. I had taken off my wings, rolled them up, and carried them under my arm. With some trouble we made our way through narrow and devious passages till we reached one of the narrow lanes running from Cannon Street to the river. Here was a little place, half public-house, half hotel, where

Dick had been lodging. He introduced me as his brother, and we shared the same room for the night.

It may be supposed that neither of us fell asleep until an early hour. I detailed the adventures that had befallen me since I left my home, and he on his side gave me a glowing description of the stirring scenes in which he had been taking part.

'We knew, though I don't think you did, Jack, what a glorious fellow old Dan is!' he cried, with enthusiasm. 'He is a born leader of men. Why, there isn't a fellow in all Ireland that doesn't fairly worship him, and he'd only have to lift his little finger to send them rushing on a battery of cannon as if they were dancing to a wedding! But even we had no idea, until it began, what a splendid fight he would make of it. He is just what Ireland has always wanted, and never had before ; and with you to help him as you can do, we will sweep the English into the sea before many weeks are over. I did my best to use the wings, but it was no use ; I couldn't catch the trick of them. But when we heard how you had been used over here, we knew you would be with us, and I made up my mind I would either help you to escape, or die in the attempt.'

'How did you manage to get over; for I have heard there is a strict blockade?'

'Oh, I came into Belfast, just after the English landed, as an Orange refugee. I shipped on board one of the transports as a fireman, and deserted as soon as we got to Fleetwood. I was awfully sorry to have to be out of it, but, after all, I knew it was the best service I could do.'

'How did you mean to get back?'

'The best chance would be to enlist in one of the regiments that are to be sent across, and desert as soon as I get a chance. The difficulty is that so many fellows have done that already that they won't take Irishmen now, and I'm afraid it won't be easy to pass myself off as anything else.'

'You must try the wings again, Dick, and a

day or two more would be well spent in teaching you. If I could not make you fly, I should despair of succeeding with anybody else. I assure you it is quite easy to anyone who has nerve and pluck, as I know you have. We will go to some quiet place for a few days, and I have no doubt you will master it if you try.'

' But think of the time lost, and the danger of your being taken again.'

' I'll take very good care not to be taken ; I will not part with my wings again. As for the time, if you learn them it will be well spent, for there will be two of us to teach instead of one when we get back to Ireland.'

In the morning we were up betimes, and after an early breakfast sallied into the streets. Nothing appeared to be known of my escape, which I calculated would not be discovered until my usual breakfast hour, about 9 A.M. Wishing to make the most of the interval, I presented myself early at the house where I had taken lodgings before my imprisonment. The landlady recognised me, but looked suspicious, and asked me where I had spent the interval. I told her I had met with a severe accident that evening, and had been in hospital until the previous day, which appeared to satisfy her, and we were allowed to go upstairs. Here I found my property untouched, and in a few minutes more Dick and I were on our way to Euston Square Station, from which we intended to book to some quiet little place in Wales. We decided on Penmaenmawr, and were on our way long before the afternoon papers announcing my escape were being cried in the streets.

We did not stay at Penmaenmawr, but were fortunate enough to find lodgings at a farmhouse some miles off among the mountains. We soon discovered some quiet spots in which we could follow our practice unobserved, and after a few trials under my direction, Dick was successful in his efforts. We did not find it necessary to spend more than two days in this occupation, and as soon as he thought he might safely venture on a long flight, we prepared to start. Our leavetaking was not very formal. As we had paid for our lodgings in advance, we did not even take the trouble of returning to the farmhouse. An hour would carry us across the channel, and we intended to have the honour of dining with the President of the Irish Republic.

Right across the channel we headed for Dublin, and I was delighted to observe how completely Dick, when once instructed in the proper method, had mastered the art of using the wings. He began to play tricks in the air, and turned a dozen somersaults like a tumbler pigeon in his ecstasy.

'Hurrah!' he shouted, 'what a benefit we'll give the enemy when we've a hundred or two fellows able to fly like this! Just fancy the effect of a shower of dynamite bombs dropped among the main body of an army, or on the deck of a ship. There's a big ironclad right below us. What fun it would be to swoop down and drop a shell into her funnel!'

'Yes—but the fun wouldn't be all on our side.

They would have fine sport making flying shots from the deck.'

' Well, of course, they will have their chance, and we must take ours. But the odds are greatly on our side. I guess they would give a good round sum if they could only get hold of us now, and use us on their side. It's a wonder they didn't bribe you and make you a friend instead of clapping you in prison.'

' You don't suppose that would have made any difference, Dick ? '

' Why, you know you did not feel like the rest of us, Jack. You always liked and admired the English, and thought us fools and madmen. Not that I ever thought you would fight against us if war actually broke out. But I think it would have been natural enough for you to take a good offer, if they had made one before the war began.'

' What would you call a good offer ? '

' Well—I don't know how such things go,' said Dick, who had probably never possessed a ten-pound note of his own in his life ; ' but I should think they might have gone as far as a thousand pounds.'

' Dick, the English Government offered me a hundred thousand pounds just after that first affair at Killynure, and that was before it could really be said there was war.'

' A hundred thousand pounds!' he echoed, in astonishment; ' and you refused it! Bravo, old fellow, that was nobly done!'

' They told me they would keep me in prison all my life if I wouldn't sell to them, sooner than let any other country get hold of it.'

' And you were ready to face that too! Why, Jack, you are as good a patriot as any of us, after all.'

' After the second battle, Dick, they offered me a million, and gave me to understand that even that did not exhaust their generosity. But it was plain, then, that the first use to be made of it was to put down the rising, and I would have died sooner than give it to them then.'

' I should think you would, and so would

any Irishman worthy of the name. Their money perish with them! But you are a hero all the same, Jack, and every man in Ireland will know how to appreciate your conduct.'

CHAPTER XV.

THE WEARING OF THE GREEN.

DUBLIN BAY was now spread out before us like a chart, and although the height from which we viewed it detracted from the picturesque beauty for which it is celebrated, I felt my heart thrill as my eye swept over the magnificent panorama it presented, from the bold promontory of Howth Head on the north, to the richly-wooded hills of Killiney and the rugged outlines of Bray Head to the south. Outside the bay, two or three English ironclads were lying at anchor; inside there was little sign of life; the hurrying steamers, the countless yachts, the fleets of fishing-boats which usually stud its waters, were no longer to be seen.

We flew lower as we neared the city ; indeed the cloud of smoke which hung above it would not only have sufficiently concealed our movements, but prevented us from steering our course to any particular point. We soon caught sight of the national flag — a huge green banner, displaying the golden sunburst and the crownless harp—which floated over the Shelbourne Hotel, in St Stephen's Green, where the President of the Republic had his residence for the present. Further to the west, we could dimly descry a crimson flag, which marked the site of the Castle, where the English garrison still held out, looking for succour from the north. On every side ruined walls and broken roofs met our view—the traces of the shells which, from a distance of four miles, were occasionally sent from the blockading vessels into the city. Out of consideration for the garrison, however, there had been no regular bombardment.

As we descended to the street, a considerable crowd began to collect, and cheer after cheer went up. Dick's expedition had been kept as great a secret as possible; but by this time everybody had heard of my exploits in London, and of my refusal to sell my invention to the English Government. It was very well known, too, on this side of the Channel, that I was an Irishman, and nearly related to the hero of the day, their commander in the north. A month ago I would have despised the homage of such a crowd. Now I thought nothing had ever sounded half so sweet to my ears as the enthusiastic cheer, swelling every moment louder and louder, with which my countrymen greeted my return to my native land. With native quickness they had grasped the situation, and a perfect roar of welcome greeted us as we alighted on the steps of the hotel. 'Welcome to Ould Ireland!' 'By the powers! we'll sack them now!' shouted a dozen voices in a breath.

'Fellow - citizens!' shouted Dick, from the uppermost step, 'it is not two hours since we

left England. Their Government offered my
brother a million of money to fight for them,
but he wouldn't have it. He has come over
to fight for his own country, and we are
just going in now to see the President. To-
morrow we hope to be with the gallant General in the north, and then you may look out
for stirring news. Three cheers for Old Ireland—hurrah!' and, amidst a tempest of applause, we stepped within the door, and asked
to be conducted to the President. A score of
eager admirers poured into the hall after us,
but at the foot of the stair a sentinel interposed his rifle crosswise, and barred their
further advance. A second soldier led us upstairs, and ushered us into a small sitting-
room, where a gentleman sat at a writing-
table, covered with papers and telegrams.

'What is that noise in the square?' he demanded. 'Have I not given orders that no
crowds are to be allowed to collect there?'

'It is my fault, sir,' said Dick, stepping forward. 'I have succeeded in my mission, and

I thought we had best come at once to you. We alighted only a moment ago at the door, and no one could have hindered a crowd gathering.'

'What! Richard!' exclaimed the President, grasping his hand. 'I hardly hoped ever to see you again. This is great news. You are welcome, indeed,' he continued, turning to me, and cordially extending his hand. 'I am delighted to meet you, and proud to claim you as a countryman. You will be worth a thousand men to us. Are these really the wings I have heard so much about?' and he proceeded to examine them with great interest, asking many questions about their construction and use.

Very little time, however, was spent in greetings or questionings. The first thing to be done was to produce as many machines as possible ; the second, to train a body of men in their use. A workshop and a number of skilled artificers were speedily placed at my disposal, and before night closed in, all arrangements were made for commencing the manufacture

N

on the following morning. We were furnished with temporary quarters at the hotel, and in the evening received an invitation to join the President at dinner. Here, around a plainly but substantially-furnished board, we met some of the principal members of the Provisional Government, and the officer commanding the National garrison,—a man of decidedly American appearance and accent, who was, nevertheless, we were given to understand, a native of Ireland. The conversation turned principally upon the new invention, and the most confident hopes were expressed of the successful results to be expected from its employment.

There had been for some time little change in the military situation. The garrison of the Castle still held out, all attempts to storm that fortress having been for so far unsuccessful, and attended by heavy loss to the besiegers. The Irish were weak in artillery, and every point of approach was commanded by field-pieces and machine-guns. So far as danger from direct attack was concerned, the garrison might be considered safe enough. On the other hand, the siege was strict, and unless relief arrived, they were certain, sooner or later, to be starved into surrender. The water supply had been long ago cut off; but it was known that they had the means of sinking deep tubular wells, and it was quite certain that they had successfully availed themselves of that power. It was not known how long their provisions would hold out ; but all agreed that they must by this time be running very short.

The possession of the new power, however, changed the aspect of affairs.

'We will try the effect of a few dynamite bombs dropped from a height upon the roofs,' said General ——. 'Three or four, judiciously placed, would probably open up the way to capitulation. If the first dose be not effective,

'rengthened and increased.'

i   ',' suggested Dick,

to a dose of the

ld be easier than

to cross over them at night and drop torpedoes on them.'

' It wouldn't do the ships much harm ; they are like turtles, and unless your torpedo is very powerful, or you can manage to explode it inside the hull, you will not do much damage. Now, I don't suppose you could carry a very heavy one up, and a light one would be no use.'

' Drop it down her funnel,' said Dick.

' You must go very close for that,' said the President, ' and it would be too risky at present. We cannot afford to run the least chance of having either of you shot. When we have a number trained, and can afford to lose men, we will let you be as venturous as you please. In the meantime, we must keep you to the less exciting work of making wings, and teaching others to use them.'

So for the next few days we sedulously devoted ourselves to this prosaic labour, finding in the midst of actual war nothing more romantic or exciting than to spend twelve hours of the day in a workshop and superintend the manufacture of machinery. My apparatus was, however, so simple and inexpensive, that in a few days a large number were turned out, and the workmen were able to go on producing them without my constant supervision. I then devoted myself to teaching the use of the wings, in which I was ably assisted by Dick. It never occurred to me that by so doing I was giving up for nothing the exclusive possession of the secret for which, but a few days before, I had refused a million. The only reward I craved was the right to be the first to show how it could be used against an enemy.

In little more than a week the nucleus of our 'flying brigade' was in existence, and ready to begin operations. It was with no little pride that I inspected them one afternoon in the great open square of St Stephen's Green. Fifty tall, active young fellows, in a smart uniform of dark green, stood drawn up in line before me. Dick acted as lieutenant and second in command. At a given word they sprang into the air, and successfully performed a number of evolutions in obedience to signals given on a whistle, amid the astonishment and applause of a dense crowd of gazers who lined the square outside the railing.   In half-an-hour the little review was over, and the men under orders to muster in College Green at nightfall.

An attack on the Castle had been determined on, and preparations were rapidly pushed on in the meantime.   The principal subsidiary operation was the erection in Dame Street, a short distance from the main entrance, of a great pole, as tall as the mast of a three-decker. To the top of this was run a large electric lamp, fitted with shades and reflectors, from which a strong beam of light could be thrown downwards on the roofs of the Castle buildings, while the upper air was left in deep shadow. It was not lighted, but left in readiness to be turned on at a given signal.

CHAPTER XVI.

TRYING A NEW WEAPON.

T the appointed hour the little squadron mustered, and I looked with some anxiety to their equipments, which were of a novel character. They carried neither rifles nor sidearms. Each man was provided with a broad belt and sling, in which were suspended three dynamite bombs weighing five pounds each. And each had a plumb-line, consisting of a leaden weight attached to a cord six feet long, to enable him to judge accurately when a given spot was exactly beneath him, so so that the bombs could be dropped with unerring aim.

We rose together, and ascended to a considerable height in the darkness. Then we moved westward, until we hovered in the air directly above the Castle. I blew a shrill note on my whistle, and the light was turned on. It streamed gloriously out, filling a broad band of space with an intense blue light, which rendered everything above invisible to those below. Every building within the walls was seen as clearly as in the broadest daylight, and looking down we could observe an unusual commotion among the sentinels. Presently the notes of a bugle rang sharply out, and the open space in front of the principal building began to fill with men, who were rapidly told off to their places, a night attack being evidently anticipated. The machine-guns commanding all the open points were manned, and strong bodies of men drawn up as much as possible within the deep shadows which extended more than half across the courtyards. From our lofty position we could clearly see everything that was passing below, while the keen glare of light, passing in apparently solid beams through the smoky atmosphere, effectually veiled our movements from the sight of those beneath us, even had it occurred to them to look for an enemy directly over their heads.

One thing, however, they did see very clearly, and that was the electric lamp by whose light we were watching their movements. One or two rifle shots were fired at it, in the hope of extinguishing it, and although they had not the effect desired, I hastened to put a stop to the firing. A group of about a dozen had been told off for this practice, and signalling my men to be ready to follow suit, I balanced myself right above them for a moment, and dropped a bomb, which struck the pavement close to their feet and burst with a loud report, enveloping the entire party in smoke and dust.

It was perhaps well that the immediate effects were thus concealed from our eyes. Shell after shell dropped in quick succession, and in a moment nothing was visible but a dim rolling cloud of dust, momentarily torn asunder by the quick flashes of the explosions.

Several fell upon the roofs, through which they crashed, and one or two walls were heard to thunder down.

When the infernal rain was over, we remained for a long time hovering in the air, waiting for the vast cloud to settle. As it slowly cleared away, a scene of desolation met our eyes. With the exception of the chapel, which we had been enjoined to spare if possible, hardly a building in the enclosure had escaped serious damage. Broken roofs and shattered walls stood up in ghastly nakedness under the glare of the electric light; below, heaps of bricks and mortar, plaster and broken glass, and bodies of men in uniform half buried among the ruins. A few forms were seen moving about in the open spaces, and shrieks and groans came up to our ears. I must confess that for a moment I sickened and shuddered at the spectacle, and was not sorry to give the word for a return.

In a few minutes we stood again in College Green. A strong body of troops had been drawn up during our absence, and now stood ready to advance to the assault, if our report should show that one was immediately advisable.

'Well, Colonel,' said the General, saluting me by a new title, 'what is the state of matters you have left behind you? Would you recommend an immediate assault?'

'It is quite unnecessary. You had better tell off a sufficient number of men with stretchers to carry the survivors of the garrison to hospital, and send four or five surgeons with them. You will probably have to force the gate, for I think there is no one left to open, much less to defend it.'

This last measure, however, proved unnecessary. While we were speaking, a number of men in scarlet uniforms, but without arms, were seen marching down the street which led from the Castle. At their head was a young officer, who carried a white flag extemporised from a ramrod and a pocket handkerchief. He was followed by about a hundred men, most of them wounded, all in soiled and torn uniforms, and all bearing a grimy, wild, and distraught appearance, such as men wear who have escaped from earthquake or other elemental danger.

The General rode forward to meet them.

'We surrender unconditionally,' said the officer. 'The most of us are either killed or wounded, and we ask you, in the name of humanity, to send assistance.'

'We will do so willingly,' replied the General. 'What will be required, in your judgment?'

'A company of sappers to dig the wounded out of the ruins, three or four surgeons to attend to the worst cases on the spot, and a body of men with stretchers to carry them away.'

While these measures were being carried out, I received a summons to attend the General, whom I found with a chart in his hand.

'The great success of your movement to-night leads me to call upon you for a further service, which will be even more glorious and important,' said he. 'I have marked on this chart the position of the three large ironclads which maintain the blockade of the town and bay. You will take half your force, leaving the other half behind, go out to the ships, and endeavour to destroy them. It is now twelve o'clock, and you have several hours of darkness yet. I leave the details of your proceeding to your own judgment, and I hope to receive a report of your success within four hours.'

I received this order with delight. I had not been one of those who accompanied the relief party to the Castle, but I could not help following them in imagination, and my fancy kept picturing the most sickening details of their ghastly work. Any active employment was better than dwelling upon the inevitable results of what I had just done.

I picked out half my men by lot, leaving the rest in charge of Dick, who was much disappointed at not being permitted to go.

' But it would never do,' he consoled him-self, ' to risk all the officers, and you are fairly entitled to the post of honour, Jack.'

Our equipment was the same as before, except that half of us carried a single ten-pound bomb instead of three five-pound ones. We followed the shore on the southern side of the bay as far as Dalkey Island, which bounds it in that direction. About a mile in the offing were visible the lights of a large steamer, the first of the line. We knew that the next one lay two miles beyond her, but from that distance we could not make out her lights.

Arrived at a point almost directly above the vessel, I halted my little party and explained my plans, which were exceedingly simple. One of the men, bearing a ten-pound bomb, was to descend cautiously until he was near enough to drop his burthen into the funnel, after which he was to rise upwards again as fast as possible. The rest were to remain in readiness to repeat the manœuvre, if it should fail the first time.

The man selected at once began the descent, and for a few moments we strained our eyes through the gloom, vainly trying to follow his movements.   Presently a slight rattle was heard; there was a bright flash, and a stunning report.   The bomb had missed the funnel, and exploded on the deck.   For a few seconds there was dead silence, then a confusion of many voices; then a shot was heard, a rocket whizzed up past us, and burst into a thousand points of dazzling brightness, which lighted up with noonday clearness an area of more than a mile.   In the unearthly glare we could plainly see our comrade hastening upwards to rejoin us.   Before the intense brightness had gone out, there was a second report, another rocket came hurtling and screaming right among us, and burst into great blazing stars above.   The effect was indescribably magnificent, but sadly disconcerting to our plans. We were confused and dazzled, and must have been plainly visible to those on board.

'Scatter, men, scatter!' I shouted, as a third

rocket came almost in the track of the second. It was plainly impossible to remain where we were ; but in spite of the flaming, sulphurous masses that were falling like a rain of fire around me, I balanced myself for a moment while I found with my plumb-line a point exactly over the ship. Then I loosed my ten-pound shell from its sling, and dropped it. I heard the crash of its fall upon the deck, and a deep muffled explosion, which told it had broken through and burst below. I did not wait to see the end, but, striking off at my utmost speed, I blew a shrill blast on my whistle to rally my followers, and held my course towards the next ship.

It was not easy now to make out her exact position. Evidently aroused by the commotion, though probably not understanding its cause, she was throwing out luminous shells on the side nearest the land. Each of these, bursting at a lofty elevation at a distance of about half-a-mile from the ship, diffused a bright light over the water, by which the smallest boat within the distance of a mile might have been distinctly seen. The rattle of a drum beating to quarters came across the water, and it was clear that she at least would not be caught napping. But while within a wide circle all was bright as day, the vessel herself lay beyond in the darkness, now denser than ever from the contrast. Her lights had all been extinguished, and the only clues to her position were the frequent flashes of her mortar, and the dull reports, as shell after shell was sent up.

This was the very thing we wanted. The darkness in which she was shrouded was necessary to our success, while the intensity of vigilance with which her crew scanned the surface of the water prevented any eye being turned towards the sky. With a low whistle I brought all my men around me, and, in a few words, directed one who carried a large shell to descend low over the vessel, and make quite sure that it dropped into the funnel. He was

o

then to shoot away to the dark side as quickly as possible. The rest of us ascended to a greater height, keeping as directly over the doomed ship as we could in the darkness.

For a few minutes, which seemed an age, we waited, looking down. No grander or more striking spectacle could be imagined than met our gaze ; the quick flashes of the mortar, the intense blaze of the bursting shells, the quivering light reflected from the illuminated circle of sea ; and, in the distance, the rockets which the other vessel continued to throw up. The third ship was now burning lights too, and so brightly was the surface of the water displayed, that even so small an object as the head of a swimmer must have been seen. But we had not long time to admire this brilliant display. We could not follow our comrade's movements in the darkness which fortunately enshrouded him ; but, after some minutes of suspense, a deep thunderous sound was heard, followed, after a few awful moments, by loud confused shouting. The firing ceased ; the light of the last shell went out like a dying lamp; and through the darkness a horrible rushing, gurgling sound came up to our ears.

'That's the last of her,' said one of the men, in awe-struck tones; 'I guess that shell has blown a hole in her bottom. Say, Captain, shall we go and try the other one? We may as well make a complete job while we're about it.'

'Yes,' I answered, feeling for the moment sick and faint with horror, and wishing I might go away anywhere from the sight of the awful blank space of sea below; 'yes, our orders are to destroy them all if we can. Follow me!' and with another note on my whistle I shaped my course in the direction of the third ship.

Whether her crew divined the fate of their comrades I cannot tell; but they immediately ceased to fire any shells or rockets, every light was extinguished, and when we fancied we had arrived at the place where she lay, no trace of of her was to be seen. It was now intensely dark, and rain began to fall; a light mist clung around us, perceptible to feeling rather than to sight. It was clear she had shifted her berth in the darkness ; and, fearing to lose our way in searching for her, I gave the signal to return. I was glad to count all my men before we started ; then, guided by the ' Pigeon ' light which gleamed almost alone through the darkness, we found ourselves back in Dublin within the four hours the General had mentioned.

St Stephen's Green was dark and deserted as I alighted at the door of the hotel, and rang for admittance. The General and the President were both asleep, but I found Dick still awake when I went up to the room which we shared together.

' God bless me, Jack, you look like a ghost ! ' was his first greeting. ' Has any misfortune happened ? Have you lost any men, or got hit yourself, or what ? '

' No, Dick ; I am safe enough. I have brought all my men back with me. I have sunk one English ship, and greatly damaged another; and I wish with all my heart you had gone out instead of me, for I feel as if I had been committing murder,' said I.

'For shame, Jack; you're as nervous as a girl. Isn't it all for the sake of Old Ireland? It's a proud man you ought to be this day, that has given you the opportunity to strike two such blows in a good cause. I didn't think anyone could ever equal Dan, but you have done it, and I'm proud to have two such brothers! Don't spoil it by whining over it like a woman.'

'I won't, Dick. I know it's a foolish weakness, and I would not say it to anyone else. But if those fellows only knew how I loathe the necessity of doing what I have done to-day! I don't pretend to feel any of the "joy of battle." I would never be a soldier for the fun of the thing—the fun of blowing men to pieces, and drowning them like rats!'

'You should see Dan,' said he, 'when the fight is hottest, how his eyes sparkle, and his hand grips his sword-hilt, and his voice rings like a trumpet, far above the loudest din of battle. It would turn a coward into a hero, only to see and hear him at such a time.'

'Well, I'm afraid I shall never be a hero, Dick,' I replied. 'The whole business is inexpressibly shocking and revolting to me. I could never bring myself to do it, if it were not that I am sure the best way to bring the whole thing to an end quickly is to strike the very hardest and heaviest blows we can while it lasts. I hate the soldier's trade from the bottom of my heart.'

'It is well, then,' said Dick, 'that you were off on another errand while we were digging the wounded out of the ruins, and getting them carried to the hospital. I can tell you it tried the nerves of many a fellow who would have faced a battery of guns without flinching. There were some gruesome sights. One fellow was dug out with almost his whole face blown away—hardly the semblance of a feature left—and yet he was alive, and the doctors say will be likely to recover. What a recovery! One

would a thousand times rather be killed out-
right! The sight of the surgeons working
away in the courtyard, with their knives, and
saws, and probes glittering under the electric
light, and their horribly cool and business-like
air, was worse than the bloodiest field of battle
could be. I can stand the smell of gunpowder
well enough, but chloroform will always sicken
me after that!'

' Did they get many out, Dick?'

' Nearly a hundred were got alive,' said Dick.
' As for the killed, they could not be counted.
You came on a head here, and a leg there, and
half a trunk somewhere else. It was ghastly.
But the men worked with a will, and if you
had heard the cheers whenever they came on
·a fellow alive, and got him out safely, you
would have thought they were searching for
their dearest friends. It reminded me of what
I had heard of scenes after colliery accidents,
when the miners were digging out fellows who
had been buried in the pits.'

' Ah,' said I, 'that would have called out my

enthusiasm far more than the fighting. After all, there is no hero on the field of battle like the surgeon in the first line of relief. He has none of the brutal excitement of fighting to keep up his courage, yet the balls are flying about him, and his duties demand the most perfect steadiness of hand and nerve. I have often thought there was no more heroic story in the annals of war than that of Arthur Landon, who was shot at Majuba Hill, and who continued his work as long as he could lift his hand, though he knew he was himself mortally wounded.'

'Ah! Majuba Hill!' exclaimed Dick. 'Do you know the Boers fought for the independence of Ireland that day? They showed what could be done against the British army by really good shooting, and set Irishmen to work to organise the body that has done such good service since. That was Dan's idea; and while you were buried in what we thought your useless dreams, we were spending every spare moment we had in rifle practice. Not at targets, or on measured ranges, but on the wild hillsides, and along the solitary shores—the crow or the curlew, as far as you can see it, is better than any target; and we learned to measure our own distance at a glance. Many a game of hide-and-seek we had with the police, and with the game-keepers; but we kept a close watch on their movements, and were generally able to baffle them.'

'Is it possible,' said I, 'that you were able to carry on such a movement under the noses of all the police that were in the country at that time?'

'Quite possible,' said Dick. 'You see they were only half-hearted. The most of them were really with us; and no wonder, when you remember the class they are drawn from. And they were afraid of us besides. It was not long till it was known well enough that there were so many dead-shots among the mountains, that they could do what they liked with the police, and that it wasn't for the good of their health to meddle with them. You saw yourself, the night Tom Crawford was shot, what an active pursuit they made! It was a rule never to shoot a policeman, unless he made himself troublesome ; and they soon came to know that well enough.'

'And all this was going on under my eyes, and I never saw it!' said I.

'Oh, you! You thought of nothing but your wings—and all the better so! I suppose a thing of that sort requires complete concentration of mind ; and, after all, you have been a hundred times more useful to us by that invention than you could have been in any other way. How I wish they would let us go north, and get to real work with it. My heart is with old Dan and his men all the time!'

'Real work!' I echoed, almost with a shudder. 'What do you call the job we did to-night? But it will be best to lose no time, and get the whole devilish business done with as soon as possible. Let's get to sleep, Dick ; it is broad daylight already, and hardly worth while to undress ;' and so saying I lay down on my bed, without taking off my clothes.

In spite of the hideous and ghastly images that kept crowding upon my mind, bodily fatigue asserted its power, and I sank into a heavy and dreamless sleep, from which I did not awake until the day was well advanced.

CHAPTER XVII.

IN THE FIELD.

WITH the morning came fresh tidings of what had been done in the night. At the first peep of dawn a boat had been sent out to reconnoitre the bay, and brought back word that, of the three ironclads that rode at anchor outside on the previous day, only one remained. This was that which had been placed nearest to Howth Head, and had escaped attack by shifting her berth in the darkness. She now lay right opposite the centre, as if to command both sides of the bay. On the eastern horizon was just visible a dark line of smoke—the last trace of the first vessel attacked, which, it was concluded, had been damaged, but not so much disabled as to prevent her from steaming away. Of the other ship no sign was visible, but none was needed to tell us her fate. She had gone down with all hands, and lay on the bottom almost exactly beneath the spot where her consort now floated. In fact, it was clear to the boat's crew that the latter was investigating the condition of the wreck, for, from a launch alongside, two or three divers were seen to go down.

In the city all was triumph and jubilation. Bells clashed in every steeple, and crowds were pouring to almost every church ; for a thanksgiving had been proclaimed by the Catholic bishops for the wonderful success of our arms in destroying the hostile garrison and raising the blockade. I must confess I did not share the devout feeling of the populace. On the contrary, I felt a thrill of horror when I found myself in the street, and realised that the hurrying crowds around me were on their way to return public thanks to Heaven for the deeds I had done during the night. I could

not join in their devotions. I made my way
among them unrecognised, till I came to what
had been 'the Castle.' Here I was known to
the officer in charge, and was admitted to gaze
on the ghastly heaps of ruins, the broken walls,
the shattered windows, the blood-stained tables
where the surgeons had been at work, and last
and worst of all, the chamber into which the
mangled bodies of the slain had been gathered
and piled in heaps, awaiting burial. What a
grim commentary it was upon the tramp of
church-going feet outside, and the joyous clang
with which the air was palpitating!

From the Castle it is but a few steps to
the Adelaide Hospital, to which many of the
wounded had been removed. Unknown to the
porter, I should have been repulsed from the
door ; but one of the surgeons, at that moment
entering, recognised me, and I went in with
him. Through ward after ward we passed, in
almost every one of which lay men with shattered limbs and mutilated bodies, some with
faces covered with dressings, the features too

horribly battered to be left exposed. I sat
down by one less seriously hurt than most of
his comrades—he had only lost his right arm
—and asked him to describe the attack as he
remembered it.

'After the first shell burst,' said he, 'it was
simply like hell. There was such a lot of dust
and smoke that everyone was blinded by it.
We couldn't tell where it was coming from.
We couldn't see anything, or tell where to
turn to, or what to do. If there had been
any enemy before us we would have charged
through it all, and thought nothing of it ; but
you might as well have tried to fight an
earthquake.'

From the wards we went to the operating-
theatre, where four surgeons had already been
busy for two hours, and had not yet nearly
finished their work. It was impossible not to
admire the scrupulous cleanliness and order
with which operation after operation was gone
through ; the absence of blood, the neat and
skilful bandaging, the swift, steady strokes of

the knife, the cool, prompt movements of the attendants, the quiet, business-like air of the whole proceedings. Hardly a word was spoken above a whisper. As fast as one patient was borne away clean and comfortable, and just recovering consciousness, another was carried in on a stretcher and placed on the table, the chloroform having been administered in an adjoining room. I had often heard the fame of the Dublin schools of surgery, and here was a proof that it was not ill deserved. There was nothing to shock the most fastidious eye ; and yet, after looking on for a few minutes, I was glad to slip out unobserved and grope my way back to the street, glad to draw a free breath again after the sickening fumes of chloroform and carbolic acid, and to see around me rosy faces and healthy bodies instead of bloodless cheeks and mutilated limbs. I had seen enough, and did not care to visit any of the other hospitals.

On returning to my quarters I received a summons to attend a council which was being

held in the President's room. It was decided
at once to send the whole available force under
my command to the assistance of our commander in the North, so as to enable him to
bring the campaign to an immediate conclusion, and I received orders to be in readiness
to start at once. Ten men were to be retained
for the purpose of making another attack that
night upon the remaining ship, and of acting
as instructors afterwards ; the rest, who now
numbered about seventy, at once prepared to
go. Already a train had been despatched to
Portadown with such baggage and ammunition
as we were likely to require. For so far the
railway line still existed. A temporary line,
which could be lifted at an hour's notice, had
been laid down as far as Lurgan, in the near
neighbourhood of which town the insurgent
general had his headquarters.

In the afternoon, however, a report was
brought in that the last remaining ship was
leaving her post, and long before sunset the
last streak of smoke had faded from the eastern

P

horizon, as she returned with tidings of mysterious disaster and defeat. What effect these would produce in England we could only guess. It might be that they would recognise the impossibility of coping successfully with an enemy armed with so irresistible a power. It was held more probable, however, that there would first be an outburst of the unreasoning rage to which the English people are periodically subject, and that no terms would be listened to until a still greater effort had been put forth and defeated.

· In that case,' said the President, ' we will carry the war into England, and send an expedition to attack them in their own strongholds. But we must first show them what to expect, by utterly destroying the force opposed to us in the North.'

We did not, of course, travel by rail. Leaving the baggage train crawling far below us along the shores of Clontarf and Malahide, we took our way northwards at a considerable elevation, travelling in two parallel lines.

' I guess we must look more like a flight of wild geese than anything else, from below,' said Dick, as we flew together at the head of the lines.

The evening was closing in as we approached the scene of conflict, of which from our lofty height we had an extended view. It did not in the least resemble a battle as one usually conceives it. No masses of men were visible anywhere ; no continuous roar of artillery, or rattle of musketry, or crash of cavalry advance was heard from any part of the wide plain on which the opposing armies were contending for mastery. And yet a hotly-contested fight was going on under our very eyes. An extent of several miles of country, from the little town of Moira on the west to that of Hillsborough on the east, was alive with knots of sharp-shooters, who lined all the wooded knolls and leafy hedgerows, and held every point that commanded a stretch of either road or dismantled railway line. The face of almost every hill was seamed and pock-marked with hastily improvised trenches and rifle pits, from which came every now and then a sharp, intermittent crackle, and light wreaths of smoke curled away and floated in a dim mist among the tree-tops. Sometimes we could see groups of men racing across the fields to seize some point of vantage, leaping hedges and ditches like hunters, spreading themselves along the cover, and pouring in their fire from new and unexpected points. But of the imposing effect of heavy masses, or even of continuous lines of men, there was not a trace. The roll of regular volleys, the thunder of the charge; everything that I had associated with the idea of a pitched battle in the field, was conspicuous by its absence; and I now realised for the first time what a change the introduction of arms of precision, and of the modern breech-loader, had forced upon military tacticians. I was now to study how I could myself best con-tribute to a further alteration; and at first I felt puzzled to imagine in what way I was to act against an enemy so impalpable and scattered. It would have been easy to attack the heavy, solid masses my imagination had pictured. But it was a very different thing to break and disorganise lines that were so broken and scattered already, or to crush bodies that could hardly be said to exist.

One point of difference, however, between the attacking and the defending forces, strongly attracted my attention. Whenever the firing grew hot at any point, and the deadly rifles of the insurgents gathered thickly, then another power was brought to bear upon them, and what the English rifles could not do was done by their artillery. From a commanding point in the distance the boom of a heavy gun would be heard, followed by the hoarse scream of a shell, dropped just behind the rebel lines, and scattering clouds of earth and stones on every side by its explosion. This usually sent the defenders running from the trenches in hot haste, to seek cover in another direction. Or, amid the loud shouting of drivers and the clatter of horses' feet, a couple of machine-guns would be seen thundering along, the great horses dragging them over hedges and ditches as if they were toys, until they reached an elevation, when in a moment they were turned about and the surrounding cover swept with a hurricane of bullets. This last was a hazardous proceeding, however, and did not always succeed. As I watched it being tried a second time upon a steep and scrubby hillside, I heard the crackle of answering rifles mingling with the shrill scream of the machine-gun. In a moment all the horses and half the men were down. The rest threw themselves upon their faces, and unslung their carbines, while the pattering of balls upon the guns and carriages could be plainly heard as a storm of shot rattled around them. Presently there was a rush from the cover, half-a-minute of close, hot work with carbine and revolver, and the guns were seized and turned upon the assailants, who in their turn were forced to retire.

This, however, was but a favourable incident ; on the whole, it was clear that the possession of artillery, notwithstanding their smaller numbers, gave the English an advantage which more than counterbalanced their marked inferiority in shooting. How I wished for a few shells, that I might silence their guns, and force them to defend their own camp and stores, and look to their line of retreat! From our position we could make out the lines of tents extending along both sides of the railway line, which had been reconstructed for so far. There were rows of temporary sheds, probably containing stores and ammunition; strings of loaded trucks; lines of defensive earthworks, and great embankments on which heavy guns were mounted. 'Here will be the scene of our operations,' I said to Dick, who accompanied me in a hasty circuit; 'we will destroy their camp and cut off their retreat, while Dan deals with them in front.'

The sun had set while we were watching the field, darkness crept over it quickly, and the sound of firing died gradually away as the light faded. We were now making for the town of Lurgan, in which Dan had his headquarters. He had been advised by telegraph of our approach, and was anxiously looking for us. His greeting was warm, but after the first hearty squeeze of the hand he turned at once to business, of which his mind was full; and we soon found he had no idea of losing a moment in the execution of his plans.

' It has been a continuous fight, such as you have seen,' said he, ' for nearly a week ; but we are taking it systematically now, and are actually beginning to sleep at nights. Let your men get some supper and an hour's rest at once ; there is plenty of work for them before morning. Your first duty will be to send a detachment down the line to blow up two or three hundred yards of it. The rest of you will destroy the trucks and stores, and as much of the camp as you can. In the meantime we will make a night attack ; it will not succeed in itself, but it will force them to show themselves in masses, when you can make short work of them.'

CHAPTER XVIII.

VICTORY.

WE did, indeed, to use Dan's terse expression, 'make short work of them;' and I am tempted to make short work also of the description of a passage in my career which, however unavoidable and perhaps justifiable it may have been, is not one which I can regard with any feelings of pride or satisfaction. That it should have fallen to me, to whom the whole business of war is unspeakably distressing and repugnant, to introduce a new and unprecedentedly destructive method of warfare, and to be the first to exemplify it in practice, is one of the most striking instances that it would be possible to imagine of what has been called 'the irony of fate.' That the necessity arose as an almost direct consequence of the peaceful scientific labours to which I had devoted myself with no other object than the general good of mankind, and the promotion, as I fondly dreamed, of peace and goodwill and universal amity among nations, is one of those moral paradoxes which perplex alike the reason and the conscience, and lead almost irresistibly to the conclusion that the evils of life result from the machinations of a capricious and malignant personality, rather than from the ordered sequence of cause and effect. My scientific training had naturally indisposed, or rather incapacitated me from recognising any supernatural agency, even in the most mysterious and inexplicable events; but when I look back on the occurrences of the period of which I now speak, and remember how foreign to my nature, how utterly unlike anything I had hoped or intended, were the scenes in which circumstances forced me to take a leading part, I can only wonder how it all came

about, and exclaim, with the author of 'Tam
o' Shanter,'—

> 'That night, a child might understand
> The de'il had business on his hand.'

I recall the whole of that dark night's work
rather as the hellish phantasmagoria of a
witch's nightmare than as a real transaction of
my sane and waking moments. And yet my
mind was never more wide awake, my intelligence never more keen and cool, than when
devising and carrying out our plans for the
complete destruction of the invading force.

It was past the full of the moon, and although the sky was clear, it was dark, as we
mustered in the market-place shortly before
midnight, and I inspected my men by torch-
light before setting out on our work of devastation. The train had arrived from Dublin with
our stores an hour before, and we found an
ample variety of choice had been provided by
the ingenuity of those by whom it had been
furnished. Every man was supplied with a
belt containing twelve dynamite cartridges of

one pound each. The whole force was then told off into squads of six, of which half were supplied with three four-pound shells per man, the rest with watering cans of petroleum, containing a gallon each. In addition every man was armed with a revolver.

We started under the quiet stars, which gave just light enough to show our way without revealing our movements, and moved down the railway line to a point below the camp. As we passed over the heads of the enemy we could see bands of navvies at work by lantern light throwing up fresh earthworks, to which the heavy guns were being shifted, in order to open fire from the most advantageous points with the first return of light. The general camp was still and quiet. The different squads passed along the lines of tents, and, as they did so, a light rain of petroleum descended upon the canvas ; the loaded railway trucks were prepared in the same way. This done, those who had borne the oil cans were directed to return and arm themselves with shells. Meantime another detachment descended on the line, placing cartridges at intervals under the rails for two or three hundred yards.

Then the signal was given, and hell at once burst forth. First, with a shattering crash, the line leaped into the air. Then the waggons caught fire, and a succession of deafening explosions announced that the stores of cartridges had been blown up. Vast showers of sparks, fragments of blazing wood, and sheets of flaming canvas and tarpaulin were hurled in all directions. In a moment the tents were involved in the conflagration, and a roaring sea of flame spread over the entire site of what had been the English camp.

It lasted only a minute, but what a minute! I have not the imagination of Dante, and I cannot picture to my readers a scene such as even the author of the 'Inferno' could not have painted, although it has never ceased to haunt my memory since. I still seem to feel the hot and suffocating rush of smoke and vapour that swept upwards to the very heavens,

forcing us to fly wildly to windward to escape
its scorching breath.   I still seem to see hurrying crowds of figures, some shining like red-hot
metal under the fierce glare, others black like
stage devils against a background of raging
flame, which leapt out and vanished into the
surrounding darkness.   I heard, thank Heaven !
no human voice to haunt me in the after years ;
every cry, if there were time to cry, was drowned
in the crackling roar of the sudden conflagration, and the crash of the explosions, as magazine after magazine went up in smoke and
thunder.   For a minute it lasted, and no longer ;
the fierce blaze went out as suddenly as it
had arisen ; the infernal roar died into blank
silence ; and of the lurid vision that in a few
seconds had burnt itself indelibly into my
brain, nothing remained except a few smouldering sparks upon the ground, and a dense black
cloud that blotted the stars from the sky.

Even at such a moment I remember remark-
ing with a certain feeling of amusement how
like huge bats were the figures that flitted round

me in the gloom, and remembering that the wings they used were of the form attributed by superstition to devils, rather than to angels. I did not forget, however, that even among the devils discipline is supposed to exist; and with a shrill note on my whistle I called my imps around me, marshalled them in order, and gave the word for a return to our quarters.

The streets of the little town were crowded with excited groups, who had seen the glare of the fire, and heard the roar of the explosions, and were filled with curiosity and anxiety to know what had happened. I kept my men together, and marched them to the railway station, where we remained to await further orders. Our success had been so rapidly and terribly complete that we were embarrassed by its very perfection, and, for the moment, found nothing left for us to do.

We were not, however, left idle very long. Dan acted with the swiftness and promptitude which were his distinguishing characteristics.

In half-an-hour I received orders to join him at a point on the line below what had been the English camp, and we at once set out. Action of any kind was a relief.

I would gladly have avoided the scene of our late exploit, but time was of consequence, and I would not for the world have betrayed feelings which would have been best expressed in the words of Macbeth — 'I am afraid to think what I have done; look on't again I dare not.' It wore a different aspect now. The waning moon, in her last quarter, had just risen, and was hanging low in the eastern horizon, where already the grey light of dawn was springing. Her level beams struck along the charred and blackened field, as if to show how complete the devastation had been. As I passed low over the ground, I feared to hear a cry or groan from some of the dark and shapeless heaps with which the plain was strewed. But not a sound or movement disturbed the silence, except a few exploring parties, who were moving about with lanterns, but who sought in vain for any sign of life. The work had been thoroughly done.

On the line below the field, however, all was life and action. Bodies of men were marching quickly in from the surrounding country, and each, as it arrived, was marshalled in its place in the long column that already extended far down on the line towards Lisburn. At the head of it I found Dan, the centre of a busy knot of officers, to whom he was rapidly giving his directions.

'This has been a glorious night!' he exclaimed, as he grasped my hand. 'The enemy is practically annihilated; you have left us nothing to do here. But our work is not finished for all that. You must go down the railway line, which they have probably reconstructed as far as Belfast. At Lisburn you will seize any trucks and locomotives that may be there, and await the arrival of the main body, which will follow at once. You will then send a detachment along the line to Belfast to see that it is clear, and pioneer the train

Q

which will be coming immediately after you. We must breakfast in Belfast this morning.'

At Lisburn, curiously enough, our little force sustained its first loss. A company had been left in charge of the railway station, and as we swept up to it in the dim light of the breaking morning, we heard the hoarse challenge of an unseen sentry below. We dashed on to seize two locomotives which stood in a siding just outside. There was a shot, and one of our men fell headlong to the ground. The next moment a loud shout was heard; men came rushing in twos and threes out of the covered station, and began hastily falling in as they arrived. They were right beneath us; but I shrank from giving the word that should destroy them. I swooped down, and alighted within a few paces of the officer who was telling them off to their places.

'Who are you, in the devil's name?' he exclaimed, in the utmost astonishment.

'I am the commander of the flying brigade of the Irish army,' I answered, 'and I call on you to surrender. Resistance is useless, for the English army has been utterly destroyed. Besides, we have you at a disadvantage. Look up; we are over your heads, and at a word we will blow you to pieces with dynamite shells.'

' We'll soon see that,' he replied, levelling his revolver. ' Surrender yourself, or I fire.'

' It will do you no good,' said I, calmly folding my arms. 'It is as I tell you. In less than ten minutes the advance guard of our army will be here, and you will find yourself outnumbered by a hundred to one. At this moment you are completely at our mercy. Be advised, and do not throw away the lives of your men in an utterly hopeless resistance.'

' Do you surrender?' he again demanded, still threatening me with the revolver.

' You may amuse yourself by considering me your prisoner for the moment, if you like,' said I. 'You will soon learn your mistake. Hark! do you hear that tramp? Here they come,' and as I spoke, the measured tread of

a large body of men began to be clearly
audible.

For a minute he looked at me with clenched
teeth and flashing eyes, and I expected every
second to feel his bullet pierce me. But it
was no longer possible to doubt the truth of
what I had said. It was plain he was hope-
lessly outnumbered, and, with a bitter curse,
he dashed the pistol to the ground, and buried
his face in his hands.

Two locomotives and about a dozen carriages and trucks were found about the station,
and as soon as steam could be got up, three
hundred men started in a train under Dan's immediate command, leaving the rest of the force
to continue their march by the road, which,
from Lisburn to Belfast, runs almost close
beside the railway line.   The flying brigade
swept down the line in advance, extended in
a long line, down which signals could be rapidly
passed.   No further obstacles were encountered,
and twenty minutes brought the train to Belfast, where the railway station was seized with-

out difficulty a second time. The surprise was complete. There was no resistance ; indeed, no body of troops capable of offering any had been left in the town. The rebels were now undisputed masters of the whole of Irish soil.

Nothing remained for the present to be done, except to deal with the ships that lay in Belfast Lough, and it was determined to pay them a visit as soon as the darkness permitted the employment of the tactics that had proved so successful in Dublin Bay. Our chief care during the day was to prevent, if possible, any suspicion of what had occurred from reaching them. No message was allowed to be sent them, and a steam tender, which was taken at the quays, was not permitted to return. In the afternoon I ascended, in order to get a 'bird's-eye view' of their position. They were four in number, anchored in a line extending across the entrance to the Lough, from Carrickfergus on the north to Clandeboye on the south. They were large ironclads, the picked vessels of the British navy, and the flagship displayed the ensign of a royal duke.

The night was dark and moonless when the expedition started. It is not my intention to give a detailed description of their work, and how it was done. There was a horrible sameness and monotony in the work of blood in which I found myself unwillingly engaged, and I would gladly hurry over the account in dry and general terms. Hating it as I did, my only aim was to do it so that it should not have to be repeated ; to strike a blow so heavy that no second should be required. It is enough to say that we succeeded. Before morning, three of the mighty fortresses that had floated so proudly on the waters lay ruined and shattered beneath them ; the fourth, sorely damaged and almost disabled, was slowly making its way across the channel. I hate to think of the brave fellows who went down into the choking brine that night, without a chance of striking a blow at the unseen, insidious foe. I have no pride in the though

that from my own hand fell the bomb that
sent to the bottom the flagship of the Channel
Fleet and her royal commander. But although
I record it without triumph, I still write it without remorse. I hate the necessity of war. I
have no pride in victory. But when men do
make war, they ought to be in earnest. Their
weapons should be the deadliest they can use;
their blows the heaviest they can deal. To say
that they may make war, indeed, but that they
must not make it too effectively; that to kill
a man with a solid bullet is legitimate, but to
wound him with an explosive one is atrocious;
that to blow your enemy to fragments with
gunpowder is civilised warfare, but to employ
dynamite for the same purpose is worthy only
of savages; is a species of cant born of the
idea that war is a magnificent game for kings
and nobles, and must be carried on under rules
that disguise its essentially revolting nature,
and prevent it from being too dangerous or
disagreeable to them.

CHAPTER XIX.

MORE DREAMS.

CIRCUMSTANCES had put into our hands a new and practically irresistible weapon, and by taking immediate advantage of it, we were able to deal such terrible and crushing blows as at once demonstrated the uselessness of persevering with the contest. When the news of the destruction of the ships in Dublin Bay was brought to London, there was a fierce outburst of rage, and a demand for instant and exemplary vengeance. But when, in rapid succession, tidings arrived of the taking of the Castle; of the complete defeat and destruction of the expedition that had been fitted out at such expense, and with so much care and fore-thought; of the loss of thousands of picked soldiers, of the most renowned general in England, of three of the most magnificent ships in the world, to say nothing of two scions of the royal house—then men held their breath in consternation, and in the in-evitable pause began to realise the hopeless-ness of the conflict.

Parliament had been hastily summoned, and legislators were flocking in from the moors of Scotland, from the salmon streams of Norway, from yachting tours in the Mediterranean, from pic-nics on the Nile and shooting parties in the Rocky Mountains. They met in hot, eager excitement, breathing out threatenings and slaughter against the audacious rebels who had dared to defy the might of England, and to use against her the utmost resources of lethal science. The Royal Speech announcing an inflexible determination to preserve the integrity of the Empire, and to assert the supremacy of the Crown in Ireland, was received with enthusiastic applause. The refusal of the Ministry to receive an envoy from the 'rebels,' or to listen to any terms short of absolute and unconditional submission, was approved and upheld. And then members went home to think.

They continued to think for several days, and the more they thought the more their enthusiasm waned. They were helped in their thinking by their constituents, and it became increasingly evident every day that the country fully recognised the uselessness of contending against such odds as had suddenly been created. It was asked on every side, What disgrace can there be in accepting the inevitable? Why not recognise the fact that the Irish have a weapon against which it is vain to fight—a weapon by which we are placed at as great a disadvantage as were the Zulus, with their assegais and ox-hide shields, when compared to our battalions with Martini-Henry rifles and Gatling guns? The sneers of other nations? They will do us no harm, for they will be uttered with the consciousness that they must themselves, in the same circumstances, have submitted to the same necessity. In short, the Radical and Republican prints, which advocated such Utopian and Socialistic (and therefore wicked) dreams as universal peace and co-operation among working-men of all countries, irrespective of the Imperial schemes of sovereigns and statesmen, were found to be unexpectedly and disgustingly popular among the masses. Public opinion had undergone one of those revolutions to which it is so subject in England, having been helped to it by the discovery that the Irish for once had shown themselves able to fight, and proved their fitness for self-government by successfully kicking their would-be governors out of the country. 'Where is the next army to come from?' was asked, but not answered. 'Are there ten thousand picked troops to be spared from holding down India and Egypt, watching Russia, and reconquering the Soudan, not to speak of another illustrious general and two more scions of royalty? And is there any reason to expect that a second expedition will be more successful than the first ? Is there a commander to be found who will undertake to land a single regiment on the island ? or, having done so, to bring back a single man alive ?'

But it is needless to dwell upon the history of matters which are so fresh in the recollection of every one of my readers that most of them could probably give a far more accurate and connected account of them than I could do myself. My object is not to recount to the public a series of events which already stand recorded in the files of all the newspapers of the last year, but to make clear what was my own attitude towards them, and my own share in them. It is not to be supposed that we in Ireland pored over the parliamentary debates, or read all the leading articles in which able editors set forth the multifarious and contradictory duties of statesmen in the crisis that had come upon them. My own short experience of parliamentary discussions had not in-

clined me to attach much importance to the
opinions and intentions of this or that political
leader, for I had learned that, as a rule, circumstances over which they have no control
mark out their course clearly enough, and that
they are usually wise enough to walk in it,
whatever their previous professions and pro-
testations may have been. So, for my own
part, I utterly disregarded all that was said or
written in England upon the revolution, and
upon the part I had taken in bringing it about.
I was told, indeed, from time to time, that in
many influential organs I was habitually described as a traitor and a murderer; as one who
had introduced a mode of warfare at which
humanity shuddered; as, in short, a fiend in
human shape and an enemy of the human race.
On the other hand, I had the consolation of
hearing that by journals of a different com-
plexion I was considered to rank among the
greatest inventors of all ages, and to have the
rare good fortune to be at the same time one of
the most illustrious patriots and benefactors of

my species. I heard myself compared at one time to Timour, to Robespierre, to O'Donovan Rossa ; at another to Wallace, to Washington, to Garibaldi ; and the one side aroused my resentment as little as the other tickled my vanity. I could only smile at the shifts to which able editors were ready to go to catch the public ear, and hope that the plain unvarnished tale which I intended soon to write, would show the world how little I deserved either the unmeasured condemnation or the extravagant praise that had been showered upon me.

In the meantime I devoted myself to the manufacture of flying machines, and to the training of men to use them.   During the weeks of discussion and negotiation that succeeded the events I have recorded in my last chapter, our force increased steadily in numbers and efficiency ; a fact which we took very good care should be known in England as well as at home.   The knowledge that the Irish leaders had at their disposal a trained flying brigade of a thousand men, and that every day was adding to its numbers, had a very salutary effect upon public opinion in adjusting the relations which were henceforth to subsist between the two countries. Those relations, as all the world knows, are not yet settled in every detail; but the principle which must govern them has been irrevocably established. No proposal for union, federation, or alliance can for a moment be entertained in which the absolute equality and autonomy of the country hitherto regarded as the weaker is not secured; and in the honour of having established and enforced that principle I may without presumption claim my share.

There is one thing that, amid all the pride and satisfaction with which I cannot but regard it, is not a little embarrassing to me; and that is the exuberant admiration and gratitude with which I find my services regarded by my countrymen. It is not that these enthusiastic republicans would almost be ready to make me their king if I should show any desire for the gilded slavery of such a position; that, I trust, would be impossible to the present advanced stage of political education of western nations. But to a man with no taste and no ambition for public life ; to one who feels that his work lies in the seclusion of the study and laboratory, and that his pleasures must be found in the quiet by-ways of travel and research, of private friendship and unostentatious independence, it is almost appalling to find that people will insist on forgetting that publicity is only an accident of his career, and an unpleasant one ; and that the most real reward they can give him is permission to retain the privacy and freedom of that unnoticed obscurity which is the blessed lot of the majority. Proud as I am of the appreciation of my countrymen, it is terrible to me to be forced to play a public part, and to be regarded as an indispensable figure in the councils of the state, under the penalty of being thought either affected or ungrateful if I refuse.

That penalty, however, I can brave, and I have no real fear that my motives will, in the

long run, be either misunderstood or misrepresented. I am at present, it is true, discharging
a duty to the State ; but it is one for which I have
no special qualification, and which many may
be found to perform more efficiently than I.
My independence is certain, for the manufacture
of machines has been left in my hands, and
the profits secured to me as far as law can
secure them ; and these bid fair to yield an
enormous and increasing income, so much beyond my wants that I intend in a few years,
if circumstances still appear to warrant such a
course, to leave the manufacture perfectly free,
or else to make it the property of the State. I
have as little wish to be a millionaire as to be a
king, and regard them as equally excrescences
upon any society approaching the ideal. I cannot understand, I even think irrational and foolish, the admiration which many people persist
in expressing for my conduct in refusing certain
pecuniary offers of the English Government.
They had no temptation—hardly any meaning,
for me. I should be miserable with such a sum

of money, and the flunkyism it would inevit-
ably gather round me.

And now, amid the comparative leisure and
quiet which has suddenly succeeded to the
brazen din of war, my mind reverts to the
peaceful dreams which filled it in the old quiet
days of study and experiment, before it was
caught and whirled away in the hideous nightmare of fire and blood from which it is now
happily awaking. Again I can sit and weave
the fancies that turned the world into a fairy-
land, and made myself the happy possessor of
Aladdin's lamp, or Fortunatus' cap. Again I
can ramble in imagination with all the free
and careless facility of a bird, lingering amid
the scenes of old romance, dreaming over
the mouldering monuments of departed glory,
mingling with the rush and roar of modern
civilisation in its most crowded haunts, or trac-
ing out the lines of its future development
among the yet untrodden solitudes of virgin
forests and the remote windings of giant rivers.
Again I can see myself following the traces of

the migration and development of tribes and peoples, seeing all that is strange and *bizarre* and unexpected in the aspect and customs of 'outlandish' races, binding into wide generalisations the results of such a comprehensive survey as had never been possible before. I cull fresh facts for science from the upper regions of the air, from the frozen solitudes of the poles, from the snowy peaks of earth's mightiest mountains, from the swarming life of tropic forests. I visit to-day old friends dwelling in the giant young cities of America ; to-morrow I drop in unexpectedly on others struggling with the primæval wildness of the Australian or New Zealand bush. I share in all the life that goes on under the sun. I trace the footsteps of British civilisation in India, of Russian civilisation in Tartary. I see everything, I sympathise with everything, I love everything.

It is a dream, I know. It will never be given to any of the sons of men to know and feel so much, to aid so signally in the forward march and progress of the race. But if it be a dream, still I will cherish it. It will not be fulfilled in me; but in my successors it may, it must be more than realised. And meanwhile it beckons me on, and, although I know that disappointments and disillusionments await me, I cannot but follow. If it fall below my hopes in some things, in others it may rise above them. Reality is always grander than fancy, as the quiet sky, with its unfathomed deeps of stars, puts to shame the painted pasteboard and glaring limelight of the stage.

So, one day, I will go forth free and unknown, to realise my old dream, and for a time my place will know me no more. What fresh adventures may await me, I know not, or whether I shall live to recount them. Of one thing only I am certain—that they will be as widely different from my anticipations as was the first reception of my invention from that which I had pictured to myself. My last duty is to leave behind me this faithful record of my labours, my hopes, my disappointments. It may be that it will disarm the hatred of those who would add, my crimes; it may be that it will cool the admiration of many who would call them patriotic services. But whatever its effect upon public opinion, I shall have the satisfaction of knowing that I have at least given them the means of arriving at a just conclusion; that I have extenuated nothing, nor set down aught in malice.

THE END.

5 C : S : 2·85.

COLSTON AND SON, PRINTERS, EDINBURGH.

CPSIA information can be obtained
at www.ICGtesting.com
Printed in the USA
LVOW04s2144150816

500517LV00011B/150/P

9 781120 123763